The NO JOCK Rule

RULE #3

ASHLEY ERIN

ALSO BY *Ashley Erin*

Visit Ashley Erin's website for information on new releases
www.ashleyerinauthor.com

You can also find her on
Facebook
www.facebook.com/authorashleyerin

Twitter
@Ashley_Erin21

Instagram
@ashleyerin21

Subject: PSYC 228: Introduction to Statistics
From: Dr. Harrison
To: Spring Session 2A

Welcome to Introduction to Statistics!
A class chatroom has been set up within Parkland's internal chat system.
Class Code: PSYC228SS2A
Log-in: Student ID and universal password

Once you have logged in, ensure you download the syllabus and all of the coursework documentation. Starting May 5th, there will be a live video lecture held every Thursday evening from 5 p.m. until 8 p.m. These lectures are crucial to your success.

As noted in the syllabus, each student has been matched with a partner. Connect with your partner as soon as possible to get a head start on your joint project. How you do this is up to you, as long as you stay within the guidelines of the syllabus. Each student shall submit an individual paper on the topic and research completed as a team.

My office hours are Tuesdays and Thursdays from 11 a.m. to 1 p.m.

Please do not hesitate to email me or to schedule an appointment should you require any assistance. While an appointment is not necessary, it does guarantee that I will have allotted time to speak with you; however, I do have an open-door policy during these hours. This will be an intensive six weeks, so it's better to ask for help early on rather than waiting until the end. All coursework is due before the final on June 23rd.

Cheers,
Dr. Harrison

CHAPTER 1

Nella

May

HARRISON'S EMAIL SITS open on my laptop, a reminder that I don't have a summer vacation like my friends. Kensi, Andie, and Lucas left this morning for Vancouver Island. Kensi is dragging them along on her annual summer vacation with her "parental units" as she calls them. The apartment is eerily quiet without her blaring music and boisterous personality.

While I have only been roommates with her for a semester, I've already forgotten what it's like to live alone. Kensi's presence is so big, the apartment feels colder without her, empty. All of the usual Kensi signs are missing. The shoes sprawling across the floor into the living room. The jacket on the back of the kitchen chair, rather than hanging in the closet by the front door. The books, tablet, laptop, and whatever other device she's using spread out on the coffee table. Everything is gone.

I almost wish she would have left her mess. I'm obsessively neat compared to her, which makes the apartment feel even emptier, lonelier. Something I never felt until I met my circle of friends. I used to like being alone, it meant no one letting you down. Now I like having people in my life, because I can count on them.

Thankfully, between this spring course, my weekly meetings with Ms. Waters, and spending every weekend in Hinton with Grace and Caterina, I shouldn't have too much time to feel the sting of my loneliness.

Sitting cross-legged on the couch, I rest my laptop on my thighs and set about getting myself organized. I create a new folder for all the class material I will undoubtedly have to download before opening my browser. I've never made use of the university's chat application before, so I bookmark it before logging in.

The layout is straightforward. All of Harrison's uploads are listed at the top. I download the syllabus and the rest of the coursework, transferring everything into the folder on my desktop.

Double-clicking the syllabus, I scroll through the typical course description, assignments, test dates, and so on, until I find the partner list he referenced in his email. Scanning through I locate my partner.

CTJ2176.

Searching the list on the right-hand side of the chatroom, I find the ID and click on it to open a new message window. Class starts Monday and Harrison wasn't lying when he said the coursework is intensive. Thankfully, I took an advanced statistics course in high school. Most of this looks like it's utilizing the same principles with a psychological focus. Pretty straightforward.

Before I can type out my message, my phone dings with a text from Kensi.

Kensi: Andie and Lucas are disgusting me. Save me.

Me: Lol. Why?

Kensi: I don't want to relive it, it's bad enough I'm going to suffer from nightmares for months after this vacation. I might even need therapy. What're you up to?

Me: Sorting out class stuff.

Kensi: Don't be a total hermit while we're gone. Socialize, go out, maybe actually go on a date for once.

Me: Don't worry, I plan on running a brothel while you're gone.

Kensi: That's my girl.

Fresh guilt fills me as I send back a smiley face. She means well when she harasses me about my non-dating life, and I *know* things would be different if she understood my situation, but she can't know. None of my friends can because I'm forced to hide that part of my life. I'm forced to hide part of me.

With a sigh, I toss my phone aside. It lands on the pile of envelopes holding more *past due* notices than anyone my age should have. Glaring at them, I throw a pillow on top of them and return to the task at hand, my fingers trembling a little as I type out the message. That pile is a constant reminder that what I'm doing here is necessary, but the anxiety seeing those bright red stamps creates is uncontrollable.

> **BNA3668:** *Hi, I'm your assigned partner for the project. I just wanted to connect with you and coordinate our schedules. I would prefer to complete this work online rather than face-to-face, if that's agreeable.*

The circle next to the ID turns green, three little dots appearing as they type out their response. I like the fact that I don't know who the person is. Maybe it's the fresh reminder of how much I keep from my friends, but the realization that I don't need to hide from whomever is on the other end of this chat the way I need to keep parts of myself secret from my friends is liberating. It's not a matter of choice with my social circle, but here I'm unrestricted.

There is no face to the seven-digit user name. No face to fill with judgement or pity if I'm honest about my life. My true life, not the life I pretend to live.

CTJ2176: I'm free any time after 11 a.m. Monday through Saturday starting next week. Sundays, I'm free all day.

BNA3668: The syllabus recommends we set aside four hours a week. I'm free anytime during the week. I've downloaded the app onto my cell, so if we need to connect over the weekend I can, but during the week is better for me.

CTJ2176: Just let me know when and I will make it work.

The circle changes to red indicating my partner has logged off.

Closing my laptop, I grab my empty laundry basket and head to the basement. The laundry room is kind of creepy; solid stone walls, no windows, and only two lights, making it dark. Thankfully, since each floor has an assigned day, I've never run into anyone in here.

I clear my clothes out of the dryer, leaning against it when my phone chimes. Kensi and Andie's smiling faces fill the screen. I wish that I could have gone with them, but even if I wasn't taking a spring course, leaving for a month and a half isn't something that is possible in my life.

Back in my apartment, I stuff my clean clothes into the waiting duffel bag, calling Grace as I gather my toothbrush and other necessities from the bathroom. Once they're all in my bag, I shut all the lights off, grab my computer, and prop myself against the wall as I shove my feet into my shoes.

"Hi, sis. I'm just leaving the apartment; I will see you and Cat in forty-five minutes." I grab my purse from the closet, digging to the bottom in search of my keys.

"Sounds good. Cat's been a little under the weather today, so can you please pick up a few things on your way over?" Grace sounds tired today. Frowning, I push aside the crushing guilt I usually feel when she's overwhelmed. Guilt is a feeling I'm familiar with. I experience it with Grace and Cat, and I experience it with my friends. It's inescapable.

"Of course. Just text me a list."

Hanging up, I exit my apartment and lock the door. As I hit the bottom floor, Carter walks in with his usual cocky swagger. My eyes dart to the floor, my heart stuttering before taking off at a thunderous pace as it shoots up into my throat, taking away my ability to speak.

I thought time would lessen his effect on me, but I haven't been that lucky. Every moment I spend with him, or near him, intensifies my attraction. An attraction that cuts so deeply that if I wasn't self-destructive and pathetic, I would find a way to shut off the feelings. But there is no off-switch for feelings. We can restrain ourselves from giving in to feelings, our choices always within our power, but that does not mean the feelings ever disappear. And in the case of Carter Jacobs, they just keep kicking me in the heart.

"Hey, Nella. Where are you headed?" His voice caresses me, it's deep tone soft as he holds the door open. I move to step through, but he stands in the doorway blocking my path. His soft cologne sends me into a flashback reel of every moment we've spent together. It's so pathetic.

Lifting my gaze, I focus on anywhere but his eyes, because whenever I consider the gorgeous blue depths I feel a debilitating mixture of anger, sadness, and longing. "I'm going to my sister's place."

"Huh. I didn't know you had a sister." He pauses, I can feel him staring at me waiting for eye contact. He moves out of my way when I continue to look at him indirectly. "Well, have a good weekend."

"You too." Slipping past him, pressing into the doorframe so I don't touch him, I walk to my car with my head held high. The urge to run is strong, but I'm not one to flee from my problems.

Although, I don't typically face them head on either. I whittle away, silently, until they're gone. My silence is one of the reasons Ms. Waters thinks I struggle with anxiety, but it's better than reaching out for help and being let down. Again.

I let myself into Grace's apartment, the tiny entrance barely able to fit me, my overnight bag, and all the things I picked up for her and Cat. Kicking off my shoes, I nudge them under the shoe rack and step around the corner into the living room. "Sorry it took me so long. I stopped at the bank."

Grace walks in from the kitchen with Caterina on her hip, smiling. "No problem."

I drop the bags onto the floor, holding my arms open. "Hi, baby girl! Come to Momma."

Cat leans away from Grace, her arms open, as she gives me the biggest smile. Grace hands me Caterina and starts collecting the bags. I hold my baby close to my chest, inhaling her sweet scent as I press kisses to her cheeks.

At fourteen months, she's trying to talk a little more and, much to Grace's dismay, walking. Her auburn hair is the same shade as my natural color, but her blue eyes are an exact match to her father's. They pierce my heart a little every time she looks at me.

Holding her in my arms feels like coming home. I sit down in the rocking chair next to the couch and cradle her to me until she starts wiggling to be free. "Dow, dow."

Setting her on her feet, I smile tiredly at Grace when she rejoins me from putting away the groceries.

"What's wrong, Nell?"

"I ran into Carter on my way out of the apartment."

Her lips purse sympathetically. While my friends all suspect my crush on Carter, Grace is the only person who knows the extent of my feelings and the reason why I can't allow myself to be involved with him.

Shrugging it off, I slide to the floor and pick up one of the giant Legos I bought for Caterina last weekend. It was a splurge, but they were on sale and I get tired of resisting buying her things because of my bank account. One day the debit machine will just start laughing at me.

"She looks like she's feeling okay."

Grace lets me change the subject. I know she won't be so easy on me tonight, after Cat's in bed.

"Yeah, she just didn't sleep well last night so she's been a little off all day. When you called she was in the middle of a nap. She's much happier now."

Remembering the envelope of cash in my pocket, I dig it out and hand it over to her. "Here, sorry it's late. Marshall didn't transfer it to me until this morning."

She counts the money, frowning when she finds an extra five hundred bucks. "Nella, what is this? You should use it to pay some of your bills."

"Grace, you moved here to be a full-time nanny to my daughter. You can barely afford rent and groceries, let alone anything for yourself. It's the least I can do considering you're my co-parent. You've made it possible for me to go to university. I will never, ever be able to repay you for this."

She drops to the ground next to me, enfolding me in her arms. This is how it's always been, the two of us. Our parents weren't bad, per se, just indifferent. Neither of us has much of a relationship with them.

Grace is six years older than me and always ensured I was looked after. After I moved out of my parents' house, prior to finding out I was pregnant, they sold everything and moved south to Palm Springs. Grace is my savior, my confidant, my best friend.

"Sweetheart, you will always have my support. No matter what. And we're getting by. It won't always be like this, one day everything won't seem so hard. Besides, you only have two more years and then you and Caterina can go anywhere you like. I may tag along, though."

"I am still figuring out what I want to do. I just want to make a decent living and not hate my job. And you know I will always want you close by. You could stay on as Caterina's nanny, or I could finally repay you and provide you with a place while you

figure out what you want."

Grace doesn't want to go to college, she travelled a bit after high school, working odd jobs to pay for her needs before coming home and trying to find her niche. We look over to where Caterina sits quietly before us, playing with her blocks. She's been an easy child since the day she was born, a blessing from a one-night stand that broke my heart.

"That sounds perfect. And I love looking after Cat. There is nothing else I would rather be doing. You know I never could find anything that kept my attention. I don't know what I'm going to do with myself once she goes to school."

I don't stop watching Cat. She's growing so quickly, and I miss so much, but I try to remind myself that it's because I'm trying to ensure she has a good and secure life. A life that will lead to our bills being paid off and a steady income that we can survive on.

Where would we be if I didn't have Grace? Probably in some low-income apartment infested with bed bugs, listening to our neighbors scream at each other, while I found some cheap daycare to provide sketchy care for Cat when I'm working some low-paying shit job that won't get us anywhere.

Knowing this doesn't make our current situation any easier. "I hate being away from her so much."

Grace looks at me empathetically and nods. "I know. You're doing the best you can under the circumstances. She knows you love her."

We chat about everything while playing with Caterina until she falls asleep mid-play. Picking her up, I hold her close as I carry her to her room and settle her into her crib. I run my fingertips over her hair, watching her sleep. As she gets older she looks more and more like her father. A blessing, and a curse.

All throughout high school I was in love with him. The quarterback of the football team, he commanded attention everywhere he went. And he was always so kind to me, at least until he left me alone in an unfamiliar bedroom after a drunken night together. When I awoke the next morning, I was alone and my heart was broken.

The sound of multiple people talking in the hallway wakes me from a deep sleep. My head is fuzzy, courtesy of the never-ending flow of liquor the night before. Clenching my eyes shut, I remember blue eyes looking at me in want.

I remember stumbling up the stairs with full lips devouring mine. Falling onto this bed. And—my eyes pop open as I sit up, grateful that my head doesn't spin with the movement. The bed is empty, the room empty.

Not even a note. Not even an acknowledgment of what happened. No "Hey, thanks for the fun night of creative sex," and it was creative.

Tears fill my eyes as I clutch the sheet tighter to my naked body. I never thought that he—that the boy I had spent so many years crushing on and who seemed to care about me—would leave me alone the morning after I gave him my virginity.

A month later I discovered I was pregnant. When I was told he wanted nothing to do with his child and practically forced me to sign a contract forbidding me from contacting him in regards to her, it obliterated me.

Just thinking about it makes me flash back to that day, makes me feel like the scared eighteen-year-old girl I once was.

He was my first. He was my only.

And this past fall he came sauntering back into my life.

CHAPTER 2

CARTER

I GATHER THE dishes and set them into the sink, waving off Ava when she insists I don't need to wash them. "You guys cooked, it's the least I can do."

I'm not entirely sure what I think of the look of surprise she gives me, but then again there are usually way more people here and the kitchen is too crowded for me to help tidy up. It strikes me that my female friends all think I just dick around all the time, which isn't entirely untrue, but it's not out of disrespect that I behave the way I do. Not really. I like to think of it as a big middle finger to my father.

Maybe I need to change my tune a little, grow the fuck up. It's not like he's impacted by my decisions, and do I want to let him influence me even if it's to do the opposite of what he told me not to? Maybe it's time to prove to my friends that I'm more than the football player who likes one night stands. Their opinion of me is more important than the jackass who paraded me around like a trophy for eighteen years.

Once I'm done in the kitchen, Ava and Peyton lay out a ton of art supplies while Dax and I go into the living room to play *Halo 4*. It doesn't take long until he's kicking my ass. My head is not in the game, a shitty day weighing on me.

When I spoke to my brother this afternoon, all I heard about for twenty minutes was how he ran into his bitch of an ex, Johanna, and she didn't even ask about Natalie. I could hear how torn up he was about it, even though she hasn't made any efforts in a year and a half. Then to top it off my controlling, pain in the ass father called to interrogate me about my summer plans which he promptly tore to bits saying I am wasting my time.

Thankfully, I don't give a rat's ass what he thinks because he is the worst kind of asshole. A rich son of a bitch who looks at his sons as status symbols. I see him maybe twice a year, and it's more than enough.

Scrubbing my hands over my face, I start another round. My game is a little better, but by the time we're done, I'm slamming my fingers on the button to start another game after losing. "Fuck."

Maybe I should have stayed home tonight, but Jaden is studying and I am not in the mood to be alone. Sighing when I lose yet another round, I toss my controller to the side and get up to grab a soda from the kitchen. Ava and Peyton glance up at me, clearly wondering why I'm having a meltdown. My hair standing on end from running my fingers through it, a scowl on my usually smiling face.

Handing Dax a drink as I pass, I drop back onto the couch and crack the top.

"Dude, where's your head at tonight?" He sets his controller on the couch with a pointed look, opening the soda. One of Andie's cats crawls all over him, kneading his legs with its tiny paws until he scratches its chin.

"Nowhere, I'm fine." That's a lie, and he knows it.

"Whatever. You know we all see through it, but no one's gonna force you to talk, even if I could." He smirks. It's true, Dax is kind of a scary ass dude, until you see him with Ava and her son, Noah, then he turns into a pile of goo.

"My dad was being a pain in the ass today." That barely scratches the surface, but it's the easiest one to go with. Dax understands having a jackass of a father. His was scum. Mine will just do whatever it takes to keep up appearances, regardless of who it hurts.

I still remember when I was stuck on the bench in my first season of football. Despite the fact it had nothing to do with my skills, I was forced to go through extra hours of training until I was on the field. That's just the way he is. It's not what's best for everyone else, it's what's best for his appearance to everyone watching.

Dax arches a brow as I sit there stewing. I don't want to spend the rest of my evening talking about my feelings with Dax, so I go to a tried and true distraction.

"How's Noah enjoying Disneyland?" The subject change works as expected. His face lights up, and he starts filling me in on everything Noah has done so far.

Tearing my napkin into pulp, I listen with half an ear. Sometimes I wish I could be someone else. Or at least not always be the guy people expect me to be.

Yeah, I'm good at football. Sure, I can pick up as many chicks as I want. But sometimes I wish people saw more to me. I wish they saw the guy who loves his niece more than anyone. Or knew about my blog and my passion for writing.

I guess they would if I allowed them to, but in my experience letting people know you too well opens you up to manipulation—case in point, my father—or to heartbreak—like my brother. Everyone sees what I want them to see, I wish there was a way to create a friendship with someone who doesn't know me personally, but could know all of me.

I wonder what it would be like.

"Has anyone talked to Nella today?" Ava and Peyton come in from the kitchen, covered in paint.

"I ran into her on my way up here. She was going to her sister's house for the weekend." Thinking about Nella makes me frustrated for a whole different reason.

She's been one of the few women who won't succumb to my charms, which I like. But I wish she would at least talk to me.

We share a circle of friends, and I've done nothing to warrant her cold shoulder. I'm nice to her, I'm courteous, and I haven't flirted outrageously with her, despite how attracted I am to her. I just don't get what her problem is.

Thinking about Nella causes that odd feeling I have every time I see her to resurface. It's that feeling you get when you see someone and you feel like you should know who they are. I can't shake it, but I've wracked my brain and still can't identify where I might know her from.

I never went to school with anyone named Nella Anderson, but I feel like I knew her before coming here. There is something about her that reminds me of someone, but I can't pinpoint who. It's frustrating as hell when you can't shake that vibe. Even more frustrating is that she won't talk to me long enough for me to bring it up in conversation.

She's under my skin. I just feel like if I wasn't the guy I pretend to be, I might get somewhere with her, but at this point she wouldn't feel like it was genuine.

"Oh yeah. She goes there every weekend." Ava nods. "She sticks around here if we have game night or whatever, but prefers to go home on the weekends."

"I didn't know she had a sister." I down the rest of my soda, letting out a loud belch.

Peyton and Ava roll their eyes as Dax chuckles.

"She keeps her family stuff pretty close to the cuff, even more than Andie did. All we know is she has a sister that she visits. Not much else." She shrugs, but my curiosity is even more piqued.

Who is this woman I can't stop thinking about? Why do I feel like I know her from somewhere? If I was into all that spiritual crap, I would think we had met in another life, but I'm positive it's from this one.

I head out after losing another game to Dax, my cell vibrating with texts from my usual booty calls, but tonight I'm just not feeling it. Truth be told, it's been a while since I've felt like a random hookup. With a sigh, I scan through the messages but don't bother replying. Instead, I hike across campus to the apartment I share with Jaden.

The night air is humid, making the evening chill a little more frigid than typical for this time of year. The campus is eerily quiet, most of the students gone for the summer.

Back home, I lock the door behind me before sliding off my shoes and peering into the living room. Jaden is passed out on the couch, his glasses askew on his face. I take them off and put them on the coffee table before he busts another pair. I don't bother trying to wake him up, I just shut the lights off and make sure his phone isn't dead in case he needs to get up in the morning. Jaden keeps weird hours sometimes, and I never know when I will wake up to an empty apartment.

Feeling my way down the dark hallway to my bedroom, I close the door behind me, relieved by the solitude of my room. My laptop sits open to the latest blog post I've been working on.

My blog, cjtalks, is about student life at Parkland. I typically write about student hacks that make life easier, upcoming events, or contests that are happening around campus. Lately, I've also been posting random opinions about different places I've been. Reviewing anything and everything from ski hills to restaurants. Rarely, I post something personal, but since no one knows it's me I feel like it's a safe place to vent.

I read through my post, making some tweaks, and then upload it onto my Tumblr page.

Stripping down to my boxers, I grab my favorite football from my desk and start tossing it in the air, Nella's chocolate brown eyes stare at me from the photo on my nightstand. The group photo was taken when we all went for a picnic this spring.

That day stands out for me because it's the one and only time Nella let her guard down and looked me in the eye. I wonder what was different about that day. Ever since I met her at Lucas's, those brown eyes have been my constant companion.

Those brown eyes that suck me in and make me question my

stance on relationships, because Nella isn't the type of girl you have a one-night stand with, she's the type of woman you commit yourself to.

Which makes my attraction to her even more terrifying. I'm not at the point in my life where I want to let someone in, where I want to hand over my heart to another person. Yet the draw is there. The intrigue. Which is why I haven't been more aggressive in my flirting, I know I could probably wear her down, but then I would be risking more than creating drama in our circle of friends.

I would be risking my heart.

I used to be less cynical, but I see what my mother's death turned my father into, a hard man with no room for anyone, although I would be willing to bet he was that way before she died. Then there is Billy, he's barely holding it together. The men in my family don't deal with loss well, and I think at my age finding "the one" is extremely rare. Between Andie and Lucas, and Dax and Ava, our group's success quotient has been filled.

Grabbing the frame, I tip it so it's face down. Being melodramatic isn't usually my vibe, but I can't seem to shake the mood of the day.

Our kitchen table wobbles as I set my stuff down. No matter how many times I adjust the legs, there is always a wobble. Grabbing a chunk of cardboard from the recycle bin we keep next to the counter, I stick it under the offending leg, testing it out. Not the best fix, but at least it's steadier than it was.

Spreading out the notes from my statistics class, I finish reading through the requirements for my project. We're to research a topic, utilizing previous studies, and examine whether our hypothesis produces significant results.

Unsure how reliable my partner will be, I've already completed the first two individual assignments to get them out of the way. They're not as difficult as I thought they would be, Harrison's video lectures are detailed and easy to follow which makes hella difference.

I open the app I downloaded for the chatroom and click on the conversation from Friday.

CTJ2176: Hey. How do we want to start this?

BNA3668: We need to come up with a hypothesis and then research previous studies that have tested it.

CTJ2176: I'm going to be honest and say that aside from an intro psych class I don't have much experience or knowledge that would be useful in coming up with a good hypothesis.

BNA3668: You're in luck. Psych is my minor and I did some preliminary research already. I've selected a couple of topics that have an abundance of peer reviewed journals.

CTJ2176: Thank god. I swear I will contribute equally to the project, I was just being up front.

BNA3668: I understand. My preference would be to examine the research on the effects of pets on stress. Analyze whether pets significantly reduce stress or if it's a myth. I'm hypothesizing that pets reduce stress.

CTJ2176: Sounds good to me.

I prop my legs up on the kitchen chair opposite from me and settle in to study for a few hours. I'm grateful my partner seems to be as motivated as I am to do well in this course. I need a statistics class to graduate. The idea of sitting in a classroom discussing a topic that doesn't interest me was something I didn't want to deal with, so I opted for an online course. The only one available was this one.

With Parkland's intensive football camp, it's not like I can go anywhere anyways, I might as well get some coursework out of the way and doing it online means I can get it done quickly. Starting Monday, my life will revolve around football and statistics. Thankfully, Dax and Ava are still here for the entire

summer, so I won't go completely insane.

As we hash out what we're looking for in different studies, agreeing to research this week, I realize that I have no idea who the person is on the other end of this chat. Smiling, I lean forward and begin to type. I can be more than a quarterback here. I can be more than a player. I can be myself.

CTJ2176: *It's a little weird not knowing your name, only seeing your student ID.*

The little dots appear before disappearing. This goes on for a solid five minutes, before her response pops up.

BNA3668: *My name is Breanne.*

Breanne. I feel a pang in my chest. An auburn-haired girl with warm, chocolate brown eyes appears in my mind. Breanne Cooper. She was often mocked and teased in high school because of her dark auburn hair, freckles, and braces. Some of the crueler girls made fun of her for being a little chubby—I always disagreed, she was curvy—and because she wore these big glasses that covered half her face. I always liked her. And I knew she was half in love with me, but I couldn't risk subjecting her to my father, he would have destroyed her, so I always kept my distance.

Except for one night. A night that I will never forget, a night that I did something I regret every day of my life.

Bre's cheeks are flushed pink as she smiles up at me, sipping at the drink in her hand. She's tucked into my side, a result of some bitch making a snide comment about the sexy as fuck dress she's wearing.

That same bitch is across the room scowling at Bre. Pretty, sweet, kind Bre. She's the only girl worth any attention at our school, and no one seems to realize it but me.

My cock twitches when she leans forward to set her empty solo cup on the table, her tit pressing into me for a teasing moment before she straightens and glances up at me again.

When her tongue darts out to lick her lips, I curl my fingers into her side a little more. The music is blaring, so loud my ears are pounding.

"Let's go over there, it's a little quieter." I jerk my chin towards the empty den at the front of the house.

Bre curls up on the couch, taking a sip from the drink in her hand. She's more relaxed than I've ever seen her, courtesy of alcohol, but she's not stumbling around drunk like the rest of our classmates.

Jerking my chin toward her cup, I ask, "How many have you had?"

"Just three. I like to get a little buzz, relax enough not to stress about what's going on, but not enough that I'm out of control."

Relaxing a bit, she tells me about her plans and I can't help but watch the way her pink lips move, glistening from her drink. She's so sweet and so gorgeous. I've wanted to kiss her since the first day I found her crying into her locker.

I've had enough to drink that my reasons for resisting don't seem important anymore.

Leaning forward, I cup her cheek. Smiling when her eyes widen, I pause to see if she pulls back. When she doesn't, I whisper, "Bre, may I kiss you?"

She licks her lips, her eyes dropping to my mouth before connecting with my gaze again. Her voice is hoarse when she speaks. "God yes."

Closing the distance between us, I kiss her gently, exploring the way she feels and tastes. Savoring her.

Bre lets out a moan and suddenly she's straddling me, deepening the kiss. I can't stop the grin from forming as I move my lips to her neck. "You never cease to surprise me."

Her breath comes out in sexy pants, my cock standing at full attention as she mindlessly grinds into me. "Carter, I want—I want you."

She leans away, her eyes flicking between mine, her lower lip caught between her teeth as she waits for me to deny her.

"Bre, are you sure? You've been drinking and I don't expect anything more."

I can see the shy girl warring with this new, braver version of Breanne, but her words are sure when she speaks. "I'm sure. I'm not drunk, I know what I want. I want you." She looks down and whispers, "It's always been you."

Closing my eyes, I grit my teeth. That was the best night of my life, and I walked away from her. Glancing at my phone, the screen is black from waiting for so long. I log back in and finally reply to Breanne.

CTJ2176: *I'm CJ.*

We finish warming up on the field, standing as our new Coach strides over, ever-present clipboard in hand.

"I'm Coach Leblanc, Coach Sanderson wanted to be here to formally introduce us; however, he had something come up. Last season we did not perform our best. That's unacceptable, and I will not be as lenient as Coach Sanderson was. This summer you will be pushed harder as a team and as players than you've ever been pushed before. There is a lot of talent here, each of you brings something to this team, and I will not accept any slacking. If you are late, the entire team will face the consequences. If you don't perform up to par, the entire team will run extra plays. By the time this camp is over, we will be prepared for the season. We will be prepared to challenge our competition and give them a run for the championship."

Diving right in, he runs us through Coach Sanderson's playbook one play at a time. We can hear grunts of disapproval, his pen scratching constantly as he makes changes. Each play is repeated, as he tweaks until he's satisfied and moves on to the next.

By the time I get home, I'm covered in dirt and grass. I have a short amount of time to clean up before I need to message Breanne about getting started on our project. Stripping down, I crank the faucet to hot and bounce on the balls of my feet while I wait for the water to heat up.

What a shitty ass practice. I'm not someone who needs to be praised constantly, but this guy communicates in grunts and it's irritating. Granted, I think I'm just not as in love with the sport as I once was. When we were hiking off the field, the majority of my team seemed to feel a sense of rejuvenation, raving about how we were challenged for the first time in over a season. If I had the energy, I would have responded but all I felt capable of doing is grunting.

Rushing through my shower, I throw on some sweats before collapsing onto the couch. I don't bother booting up my laptop, opening the Parkland Chat app on my cell instead.

CTJ2176: *Sorry I'm late . . . work ran long.*

I don't specify what work is, I like that I'm more than a number on a jersey with her. I feel guilty though, I'm going to be constantly late if today is an indication of how practice is going to go. Coach decided we couldn't call it a day until the play was perfect and it was the first day.

I wait for Breanne to log in, flipping through my notes. We're a week into the project, and while we haven't branched out into our personal lives, there is something liberating about being completely anonymous.

She doesn't know what I look like. Or that I'm a quarterback. She doesn't know I inherited five hundred grand when I turned eighteen. What she will know is that I write a blog. That I have a niece I adore. And any other part of me I want to share. All the parts I always keep hidden.

It feels kind of awesome to talk to a chick who knows a different side to me than the persona around school. Something real. Like testing the waters.

Setting my phone down when she doesn't respond immediately, I gather my dirty clothes and run down to the basement to the laundry room. By the time I'm back on the couch, thirty minutes have passed and she still hasn't responded.

CTJ2176: *Breanne? Are you okay?*

She's usually the first to message me in the day and when I don't hear from her within two hours of getting home I start to worry. I shove my cell into my back pocket before joining Jaden in the kitchen.

"When do you head to your parents?" I take the plate Jaden hands to me, helping myself to two chicken breasts, a mound of rice, and filling the rest of my plate with asparagus. I'm starving, and even though I inhaled a power bar after practice I'm grateful Jaden cooked a late lunch.

"Tomorrow."

We sit at the kitchen table and eat in silence. Jaden is reading, and not a novel. He's reading a fucking textbook from one of the classes he starts in September. I guess that's how he rocks a 4.0 GPA. The guy could be anything he wants to be, he's that smart.

He's the only one in our circle of friends who knows about cjtalks, my dad, my brother, and every other detail about my life. Jaden and I met during a tour of the university prior to attending and just clicked. He's a solid guy who keeps mostly to himself, aside from our circle of friends. He's quiet, doesn't talk about himself much, but he's easy to live with and calls me out when I'm being a dick. Aside from my brother, he's the only real family I have.

My phone beeps at me. It's the tone I set for Parkland Chat. Dropping my fork, I snatch it out of my pocket, almost dropping it in my haste.

"Booty call?" Jaden marks his spot with his finger, looking up at me. There is no judgment, but I know he's worried about me. The New Year did not bring about the best decisions, and winter semester I made more than one mistake in my choice of a bedmate. One of the reasons I've pulled back from random hookups.

"No, my statistics partner finally got back to me."

"Huh. I didn't know you cared about statistics this much. Potential hookup?"

I feel the need to defend myself, even though I know Jaden isn't trying to make me feel like shit.

"Nah, I'm kind of over that. Too much trouble getting them

24

to leave like they promise. I do like that she doesn't know who I am. I can be myself."

"You can be yourself around the rest of our friends, you just choose not to," Jaden replies as he returns to his reading.

Ignoring him, I tap the app logo and open my chat window with Breanne.

BNA3668: *I'm sorry. It's been a shitty day.*

CTJ2176: *What's wrong?*

I stare at my phone for a good ten minutes before she starts to type out a response.

BNA3668: *My daughter had a severe allergic reaction to a plum. I don't think I've ever been so scared in my life.*

Daughter?

CTJ2176: *Daughter? Poor kid. I know how that feels. I'm severely allergic to plums and apricots, and I remember my eyes swelling shut when we discovered the allergy. Oddly enough, I was five at the time. Who doesn't try a plum or an apricot until they're five?*

BNA3668: *Yeah, she's almost 15 months. I got pregnant when I was 18, she was born three months before I turned 19. She's fine now, sleeping. I'm sorry for taking so long to respond, I had to drive back to school and when I got to my apartment my laptop was dead and my cell was close to dead.*

CTJ2176: *Hey, priorities. I get it. My brother is a single parent; he would ignore the world for my niece. Although she's so damn cute I'm sure the world stops when she walks into a room. If you need to be with her tonight, we can always take the night off.*

BNA3668: *She's with my sister in Hinton. It's complicated–you have a niece?*

CTJ2176: Yeah. She owns me. LOL.

BNA3668: You're a protective uncle, aren't you?

CTJ2176: Right now, I'm the fun uncle. When she hits puberty, I may have to make some friends in law enforcement to keep me out of jail.

BNA3668: I just laughed out loud. Thank you, CJ. I needed to laugh. I'm not feeling up to this tonight. I will text you tomorrow.

She signs off before I can respond. Staring blankly at the screen, several minutes' pass before I set my phone down on the table and pick up my fork to scarf down my now cold dinner.

The wheels in my head spin, where is the girl's father? I hate absent parents. I grew up with one. I watch my brother struggle with being a single parent and he's got a good job. Breanne is not quite twenty, I can't imagine how tough it is on her.

I saw how much Ava struggled until Joe stepped up. There is only one excuse for a father not to be there for his child, and that's death. It's harsh, but it's the truth.

I look up as Jaden stands, washing his dishes before disappearing into his room. He doesn't question me any further about why I choose to keep parts of myself from our friends. That's one of the things I appreciate about living with him, he says what he needs to say and then he drops it. I hate when people continue to pick at an issue, it makes me want to dig my heels in and do the opposite of what they say. A knee-jerk reaction from my childhood with my father.

CHAPTER 3

BNA3668: *I've attached my notes from the studies I collected. I'm just finishing up working through the initial numbers.*

CTJ2176: *I just have one more study to review. I got my ass kicked at work, my boss screamed at me and my coworkers were dragged down with me, it set me behind. Anyway, I think Harrison will like the fact that we are comparing opposing studies. The evaluation will help get more conclusive results.*

BNA3668: *I'm sorry to hear that work sucked. Why did he yell at you?*

CTJ2176: *It's not important.*

BNA3668: *If you say so.*

CTJ2176: *How's your paper coming?*

BNA3668: *I'm done. My roommate is out of town; it leaves me a lot of spare time during the week. I hate having homework on the weekend, that's my time with my sister and Caterina. What about you?*

CTJ2176: *I just have the final argument and then I will be done as well. Caterina? That's a pretty name.*

BNA3668: *Thank you. She's going to be a ballbuster when she gets older, which I like.*

CTJ2176: *What does her father think of that?*

BNA3668: *He's never met her. I'm not even allowed to contact him about her.*

CTJ2176: *Seriously?*

BNA3668: *Yeah, the mistakes we make when we're young.*

CTJ2176: *What a piece of shit. I would be harassing him every damn day.*

BNA3668: *It's complicated. I signed a contract agreeing not to in return for a hefty child support payment. If I break the agreement, I must pay every penny back. I can't afford that, I'm swimming in debt as it is. Like I said, hindsight is twenty-twenty to the mistakes we make.*

CTJ2176: *Wow. That sucks.*

CHAPTER 4

Nella

LEANING ME BACK against the wall, I close my eyes and focus on my breathing. Tears run down my cheeks as I fight the anxiety dealing with Marshall always gives me.

He is such an asshole.

The threat is never blatant, but it's there every time I broach the subject of Cat meeting her father. The tone he gives me when he explains how generous my child support is and how if I'm going to harass him about the conditions he may need to re-evaluate his generosity.

Generous my ass. I see it for what it is: a pay-off to keep me silent.

The man is bigger than life and everything about him scares me, including his ability to make me lose everything. I suspect even my scholarship if he wanted to.

My heart finally slows to the point I feel ready to proceed, so I enter the reception area of Parkland's three on site counselors.

Ms. Waters' door is open, so I let myself in after swiping my sleeve over my damp eyes.

"Ah, Nella. It's good to see you again." She smiles at me from behind her desk, her eyes crinkling in the corners.

I take my usual seat, ready for another unbearable hour where I try to find the courage to ask for the help I need. It's not that I don't like her. It's not that she's not good at her job. It's that I'm not good at admitting maybe I'm not capable of dealing with everything on my own. The last time I asked for help didn't go well for me, in fact it's the entire reason for my anxiety. I'm not stupid enough to think that Ms. Waters is in the same realm as Marshall, but anxiety has no reason.

In fact, I like Ms. Waters, she's warm and kind. She's intelligent. If she were a professor, I would enjoy listening to her speak, but under the circumstances I wish I didn't need to see her. The only reason I come here for one hour a week is because of the anxiety attack I had in the middle of class mid-semester. Not that the school is forcing me to be here, but in that moment, I couldn't think of a reason not to come.

I haven't had one since, thank goodness, but I feel the weight of the past two and a half years on my shoulders. The guilt is suffocating, and I don't even know how to begin explaining why I feel guilty when everyone who knows my situation tells me I'm being ridiculous.

"Hello."

"Before we begin, I have an idea I want to run by you. I know you don't find our time together overly useful, and I understand. Talk therapy doesn't work for everyone." She stands and walks around her desk, handing me some papers.

Hyatt Equine Therapy. As I read, I realize it's not therapy for people, but different holistic therapies for horses.

"I don't understand."

"Nella, I don't think you're ready to really delve into the reason behind your anxiety attack. I've contacted Lia Hyatt, the owner of HET, and she is interested in taking on an assistant. I've done some extensive research on the benefits of working with animals and the impact on anxiety. I think this is worth a try. Whatever is at the root of the way your body needs to cope with the overwhelming feelings, doing something like this may help."

I read through the description of services offered and the emails already exchanged between Ms. Waters and Lia Hyatt. The studies I've been reading for my statistics class come to mind. I don't typically believe in coincidences, so I take the suggestion seriously.

I've never been around horses before, but when I see a photo of Lia with a horse there is something that draws me to her. I read her bio and feel a kinship with her. She looks kind and calming, and she's outside my social group so I would be able to open up to her.

"Okay. I think it sounds like a good opportunity."

"I will make the arrangements and forward you the information."

Later that night, I'm visiting with Dax and Ava when Carter walks into their apartment, his piercing blue gaze honing in on where I sit. Dax and Ava are cuddling on the love seat, which only leaves the spot next to me available. Tucking my legs against my chest, I resist the urge to move.

I miss the rest of our friends. This feels too intimate. A group is safer, I can melt into the background. That's not possible right now and it's causing my anxiety and shame to rear its ugly head.

The couch dips as Carter sits next to me. I meet his eyes, before quickly glancing away. The look is always the same when he sees me, attraction and curiosity. What's missing is recognition.

How can you not recognize me? I want to scream at him.

How can you not remember me? Or walk around without feeling any remorse at impregnating me after one drunken night together and forcing me to sign a contract that states I can't approach you about our daughter?

I remember sitting in the doctor's office, young and pregnant, while a couple stared at me enviously. They were there for fertility treatments—I overheard the receptionist talking to them. I could see the wish in their eyes. The knowing looks they threw my way. A young, pregnant girl who was there alone. Compared to a vibrant couple who was clearly more prepared for parenthood. It's interesting how fate works. Sometimes she's a real bitch.

I completed my first year of Parkland through their distance learning program. I wrote them several letters and completed an in-person panel interview before they would agree to allow my scholarship to transfer to that program rather than on-campus.

All of that I tackled on my own. Grace was there as much as she could be, but it's different than having the support of the person who should be there for you.

I take a slow, deep breath, trying to calm the racing of my heart.

My emotions stir up as his intoxicating scent invades my senses.

Hurt, anger, heartbreak, attraction, love, regret.

I've been in love with Carter Jacobs since I was known as Breanne Nella Cooper. After high school, I changed my last name to Anderson, the surname of my maternal grandmother, because I always felt more of a kinship with her than my parents. It was a naive thought that by changing my name I could change my life.

I dropped the Breanne and became Nella Anderson. I wanted to leave that part of my life behind, but I'm still that girl. The girl whose heart belongs to someone who doesn't deserve it. The girl who can't share a part of who she is because she was young and foolish, desperate when a stack of papers was thrust under her nose by an imposing and cruel man. A girl who didn't know how to fight for what was right.

With a new name and changed appearance, I look different but I don't feel any different. I'm still the same girl. I still love the same boy. He just doesn't love me back, because if he did, all that surface stuff wouldn't matter. Our souls would recognize each other.

Me: Why do I still love him?

Grace: We have little control over how our heart feels, even when our head tells us it's a bad idea.

Me: Stupid heart.

Grace: Talk to him . . .

Me: I can't. If I break the contract, I need to pay back every penny I've been given for Caterina and all future support will be terminated. I can't afford that. My bank account is in the negative right now.

Grace: Can't you talk to Marshall about renegotiating the contract?

Me: I just tried to today and it sent me into a near panic attack. Marshall Jacobs does not renegotiate. I should never have signed that damn piece of paper.

Grace: Why don't you come home early this week? Sounds like you need a pint of ice cream and the company of the best sister and daughter in the world.

Me: Yeah, I think I will.

Returning my attention to the conversation surrounding me, I try to enjoy the company of my friends. Ava and Dax are telling us about Noah's trip to Disneyland with his dad.

Carter's smirking as they talk, which makes me want to throttle him. How can he sit there and grin? How can he not think about the daughter he doesn't know?

I'm envious of Ava. Joe wasn't there for Ava and Noah for like five years, but he's stepping up now. I'm so happy for her, but I wish I had the same faith that things would turn around for me and Cat too. I just don't when I see the amusement on Carter's face.

Knowing that Ava has gone through this makes me wish I could talk to her about everything. It takes me a while to open up about myself to strangers, but Carter being a part of my social group puts a kink in what I can share. I thought attending Parkland would give me enough distance, how wrong I was.

I wish Ava and I could do playdates with Noah and Cat. Or that we could talk about parenting. I wish I could tell Andie and Kensi about my sweet girl.

Keeping secrets sucks. The rules that confine me are ones I never anticipated. They say hindsight is twenty-twenty, and it's true, just like I said to CJ.

"Earth to Nella." Ava waves her hands out in front of her, smiling as I blink a couple times before focusing on her.

"Yeah?"

"Where did you disappear off to?"

I resist looking at Carter. "Umm, I got offered an internship today. I was just contemplating my schedule and how to fit it in."

"That's so cool. Doing what?"

I can feel Dax and Carter's eyes on me. My face heats up with all the attention, but I focus on Ava.

"I will be assisting a woman who does equine therapy."

They listen as I explain what I know until I finally change the subject back to them by asking about their wedding plans.

CHAPTER 5

BNA3668: *I'm a shitty parent.*

CTJ2176: *No, Cat's father is a shitty parent. You're doing what you need to provide a good life for your kid. That takes guts.*

BNA3668: *I guess . . .*

CTJ2176: *Shitty parents don't say, "I'm a shitty parent."*

BNA3668: *I just want what's best for her, but I question every decision I make. Maybe I should drop out and find a job. I spend five nights a week away from her.*

CTJ2176: *Bre, try not to think of it that way. Think of it more like you work out of town. There are lots of parents who work out of town during the week. This isn't forever.*

BNA3668: *You're not the first to point that out. I guess when I think of a parent working out of town I think of dads not being there. I know I need to change the way I think; it's just hard leaving her. So . . . I read your latest blog post.*

CTJ2176: *You and like three other people.*

BNA3668: *Try most of Parkland's student body. Your blog was pinned on Parkland's Facebook page. The entire thread of comments was trying to figure out who you are.*

CTJ2176: Creepy. I like being anonymous. It's easier to be myself through a keyboard than in person. People have all these expectations of me in real life. They expect me to act a certain way, focus on specific things. It's exhausting.

BNA3668: I know what you mean, I feel the same way. There are just some things I can't talk about.

CTJ2176: Well, now you can talk to me.

BNA3668: Ditto.

cjtalks

At times, it sucks being one of a couple hundred students sticking around campus all summer long. All our friends are off doing road trips, family vacations, or summer internships. And here we are, completing spring or summer classes with nothing better to do than hang around campus.

I have good news for you! Parkland will be offering a Cinema in the Park on Sunday evenings until the end of August. Write in to studentlife@parklanduni.com to submit your suggestions.

This Sunday at 9:00 p.m. come watch *Guardians of the Galaxy*.

Location: Lowe Science Building, on the west side.

Bring your blankets or lawn chairs.

I will be there, will you?

#parklanduniversity #studentlife #cjtalks

CTJ2176: Are you going to the Cinema in the Park?

BNA3668: Yeah, my friends are dragging me along. I need to leave Hinton early, but I promised I would go.

CTJ2176: It's going to be awesome, why aren't you more excited?

BNA3668: *There is this guy, it's just tough to be around him and he's friends with my friends.*

CTJ2176: *I take it this guy is a jerk?*

BNA3668: *We have a tricky history, and he doesn't seem to remember. It's okay, I just keep my distance.*

CTJ2176: *What's his name? I'll kick his ass.*

BNA3668: *Lol*

CTJ2176: *I'm not joking.*

BNA3668: *Thank you, but it's unnecessary.*

CHAPTER 6

Nella

THE LAWN OUTSIDE the Lowe Science Building is filling up, it seems every student still on campus is here. I scan the crowd, wondering where CJ is sitting. We're halfway through statistics, our papers are done and there is no reason to still talk to him, but instead we talk more than ever.

There is something about him that draws me out of my shell. I've always been on the quiet side, but lately I find myself retreating even more. I don't want to lose myself, I want to be strong and confident. I don't want to miss out on life and love and adventure because I'm scared.

It's time to face my demons. Talking to CJ helps give me perspective, he has a way of phrasing things that gives me courage.

"This is pretty cool. I wonder if CJ organized it with the school." Ava sits next to me, checking things out. Grinning, I sip my iced tea. My friends don't know my statistics partner is the infamous CJ from cjtalks. He entrusted me with that knowledge and I won't break his trust. That doesn't mean I didn't ask him about this new development, and while he denies any involvement he seems to be a pretty modest guy so I doubt he would admit to having the idea.

"It's quite the mystery, isn't it?" Peyton joins in. "His blog just popped up, what a month or two ago, and it's huge."

I burst with pride for my friend. Someone I've never met in person, but who knows me almost better than anyone else in my life outside Grace.

"Hey guys." Carter walks up with a couple of his football buddies. We look between the two guys, they're identical twins and I picture what Kensi would do if she was here. It makes me miss her. "This is Chase and Grayden. I hope you don't mind if they join us."

The screen is blank, the oranges and pinks of the sunset blanketing us in its glow as the guys sit down, their massive size makes the large blanket crowded as we all squish to make room. Dax and Ava are curled up together, Peyton sitting next to Dax on the edge of the blanket. Once again, the only space open is next to me, and, of course, Carter snags that spot. The two hulking football players he invited to join us create a wall of heat at the back of the blanket.

> **Me:** Your head is about to explode.
>
> Kensi: Why?
>
> **Me:** Carter brought two of his football friends to this Cinema in the Park thing. They're TWINS.
>
> **Kensi:** I need a picture.
>
> **Me:** That's not going to happen.
>
> **Kensi:** I dare you.
>
> **Me:** I'm not Andie, that's not going to work with me.
>
> **Kensi:** C'mon. I've been enduring the worst string of dates known to man. I need something to think about at night.
>
> **Me:** Tell me about these dates.
>
> **Kensi:** Nothing worth telling. I have the worst taste in men.

Me: You always go for the out of reach guys. The complicated guys. Why not try dating someone your own age?

Kensi: Boring.

Me: You're a ridiculous person.

Kensi: And yet you love me.

It's a struggle to breathe with so many people surrounding me, especially with Carter's arm brushing against mine. I swallow hard, counting my breaths to calm my racing heart.

I wasn't an anxious person until Carter Jacobs walked back into my life, but the strain of keeping my secret has become unbearable, it makes me feel like I'm choking. I feel guilty that he doesn't remember me, that he doesn't know his daughter. Completely ridiculous considering he is the one who made the choice not to be involved with her. Top the guilt off with the fear that his father will take away my only means of providing for my daughter if he ever finds out Carter is in my life, it's a wonder I have managed to get through each day with some measure of composure.

As the night cools off, I wrap my arms around my legs, goosebumps pebbling across my skin. I jump when I feel hands setting something across my shoulders. Looking down, I finger the gray material of the hoodie now covering me before meeting Carter's bright blue gaze in the dim light of the movie.

I can't look away, searching his eyes for something that tells me the sweet guy from high school that would say hello to me in the hall is still there somewhere. The guy who would shield me from the bullies who made fun of my body and glasses and hair and braces. The guy I fell in love with before he tore my heart out.

I believe people can change, I certainly have. Physically and emotionally, I'm not the same girl I once was. I got contacts. I started working out. I changed my hair. I'm confronting my anxiety in my own way, and trying to find the courage to take what I want from life.

Maybe it's possible that he's come around, he's not an eighteen-year-old kid fresh out of high school anymore and he sees how happy Dax is with Ava and Noah. Just *maybe*.

Whispering "thank you," I pull the soft material around myself a little tighter, allowing his scent to consume me for the moment. For tonight, I will let myself imagine things were different, to think that the *maybe* is a possibility.

Every so often I picture what our life would be like if he had chosen to be involved with Caterina. Would we be a couple? Or would we only see each other and talk to each other about Cat?

Or how different things would be if I woke up to him still being next to me. Would we have become something more? Or was it a drunken impulse, something he did because he knew how badly I wanted it?

So many questions. Questions that I shouldn't dwell on. Isn't that one of the flaws of the human condition, though? We tend to dwell on things we can't change. The only thing we have any power over is our actions in the moment.

He smiles at me and I let myself smile in return before turning back to the screen.

The movie passes in a blur, the warmth of Carter's sweater reminding me of what it felt like to be held by him. I ache for what could have been. I cherish the gift he unknowingly bestowed upon me. And I grieve the sweet, innocent girl I lost in the months following that night.

My friends remain seated when the credits start rolling, Peyton chatting with Carter's football buddies while Ava and Dax whisper to each other.

I glance at Carter from the corner of my eye, he's watching me intently. That familiar look of frustration on his face. Dropping his hoodie from my shoulders, I hand it to him. He opens his mouth, but before he can speak my cell rings, interrupting him.

It's Marshall.

"Hello?" I walk away from my friends, from Carter, anxiety building in my chest as my heart threatens to pound its way out.

"Breanne, I saw something disturbing today when I was checking out my son's Facebook profile. You didn't inform me that you were part of the same social circle." His voice is hard. It sends shivers down my spine, the same shivers you get when it's dark outside and someone is walking behind you. That uneasy sense to protect yourself from imminent danger.

I look over my shoulder to see Carter watching me. Dragging a toe through the grass, I cross one arm over my chest to grip the other arm. "Don't worry, he doesn't recognize me. I haven't broken the contract. But—I was thinking, it's almost been two years, can you check with him, see if he is interested in reconsidering being involved in Caterina's life?"

There is a hefty sigh on the other line, the sound settles a heavy weight on my shoulders and my vision goes hazy. "Didn't we discuss this recently?"

"I just—I think maybe he might change his mind." My voice is meek, unable to find its strength when I'm dealing with this imposing man.

"Fine, but you're just setting yourself up for disappointment. Carter is going places and he's not going to want a child holding him back."

A tear falls down my cheek. Mumbling a goodbye, I hang up and wipe my eyes. Taking a deep breath, I send Ava a quick text telling her I'm going home. I don't look back as I push my way through the crowd of students.

The walk is a blur; I lock my door behind me and go through the motions of getting ready for bed.

The echo of my knock on the heavy mahogany door is loud in the quiet of the afternoon. Rocking back on my heels, I hug myself as I wait. It took me all morning to find the courage to drive here, and the urge to vomit is strong—although that could be the hormones.

When the door swings open and reveals a tall man with salt and pepper hair, frown lines, and vicious gray eyes, I barely contain the urge to cringe.

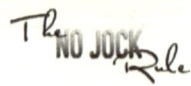

"Yes?"

"Um, yeah, hi. Is Carter home? I'm Breanne, a friend of his from school and I need to talk to him." My voice is surprisingly steady considering the weight of Mr. Jacobs gaze.

His eyes glance down to the pregnancy test I had unconsciously pulled from my pocket, narrowing as he steps out onto the concrete landing. "He's not home."

Jamming the test back in my pocket, I straighten my shoulders and meet his glare. "When will he be home?"

"He won't. He's off gallivanting with his friends before he goes to university. I will pass your—message on to him." He backs into the house and slams the door without another word.

Splashing water on my face, I stare in the mirror as the water flows down my face. When I didn't hear from him within a week, I went back only to have a contract shoved in my face with a threat that I wouldn't get any better and if I sought out Carter I would get nothing. With the rest of my heart shattering, I signed and left with my first check.

Regrets.

CTJ2176: *I need a woman's opinion.*

BNA3668: *Shoot.*

CJ's message comes in as I finish washing my face. After my discussion with Marshall, I thought about messaging him, but I wanted to get home and ready for bed first. Take a moment to get my nerves in check.

CTJ2176: *Okay, here goes. I'm not proud of my dating history. I've only cared about one girl, and I know without a doubt that I hurt her in an unforgivable way. I see my friends meeting people and moving forward with their lives, but I don't know if I can.*

BNA3668: *It sounds like you need to deal with the woman you hurt in the past before you can feel ready now. I'm somewhat of an expert at letting someone from my past haunt me, I see* *him all the time, it's unavoidable, but at some point we need to move on. Forgive ourselves, forgive them.*

CTJ2176: *How can you be so understanding?*

BNA3668: *I fell in love with one of the most popular guys in school, like many girls do. Maybe I am starting to think I was naive to believe that one night meant anything. I can forgive him for that.*

CTJ2176: *You're an incredible person. Maybe I will try to contact the girl from my past, make amends.*

We talk late into the night. I feel bad for him, his fear of turning into his father or brother apparent in what he shares with me. Isn't it ironic, we both have these irrational fears hanging over our heads? His fear of letting someone in. My fear of being a terrible mother. These feelings rule our lives in similar ways despite our differences.

It's funny, he's kind of a player, but I can tell that he doesn't like that part of his life. He just needs to meet the right woman. If I can look past that with him, why does it bother me so much when Carter runs off for his booty calls?

Because you're not in love with CJ.

CHAPTER 7

CARTER

"AGAIN!" COACH BARKS as we finish the circuit he just had us run through.

A collective groan erupts as we turn, but his shout has us turning back to him.

"Stop acting like petulant children. This camp is to make you the best players you can be. If you don't want to work hard then get off my field. For every one of you, there are five guys who want your spot. They may not have your raw talent, but they will put in the work. Talent only goes so far without the commitment to improving." He gestures towards the end zone, done with us.

Grayden chuckles as we walk. "He's one tough bastard, but I am noticing an improvement. Not to mention my abs are tighter than ever."

Chase rolls his eyes, "All well and good, but my entire freezer is filled with ice. I've never been so sore."

Laughing as they rib on each other, I line up behind my teammates as we go through the circuit for the ninth time. My body is covered in sweat, dirt, and grass stains.

He seems satisfied by the time the last one of us is done, dismissing us with a grunt. The team makes its way to the locker room without the usual banter. We're all too damn tired.

Collapsing onto the bench by my locker, I reach inside and grab my towel. Instead of leaving like he has since day one, he follows us into the room, standing in the center and evaluating the exhausted silence.

Rubbing the towel over my head, I faintly hear coach start giving us a lecture. It's the same as usual. We need to get our asses in gear if we're going to have a chance once the season starts in September. Blah, blah, blah.

I remember when I was one of the guys listening with rapt attention, but right now I'm barely listening. The passion for these speeches, for the game and need to win, has been missing for longer than I care to acknowledge. I know I'm not going to get away with it with Leblanc like I did with Sanderson.

Coach finally leaves us after rambling on for thirty minutes. Running my hand through my hair, I sigh. At one time, football was my life. Now it's a way to fill the time. Sure, I'm a decently talented quarterback. And yes, I love being a part of a cohesive team. It just doesn't hold the same draw anymore. I would rather work with the guys outside of the field than play.

After rushing through my shower, I hit the road to go see Billy and Natalie. The drive is long, just under two hours, but I try to make it out every couple of weeks.

Natalie's laughter greets me as I round the house to the backyard. Billy is chasing her around on all fours, growling at her. She stumbles and falls, rolling onto her back.

Billy bends down and blows on her belly, her screeching laughter getting even louder. Natalie sees me, pushes her dad out of the way and rushes towards me. "Unca!"

I scoop her up into my arms, swinging her in a circle. "You grow smarter and more beautiful every day."

She clings to me as Billy stands and brushes his knees off. He smacks me on my shoulder as we walk into the house, his hand squeezing before it falls away. It's his typical "everything will work out" gesture, which means he already knows I'm not feeling like myself. I set Natalie down so she can go play with her toys before helping myself to a glass of water.

Billy sits across from me at the table, watching Natalie bring toy after toy into the kitchen. He looks exhausted, and incredibly sad. Aren't we quite the pair?

"You doing okay?" He nods, but I cock an eyebrow and wait.

"Mostly. Johanna sent me the paperwork relinquishing any rights to Natalie. I thought it would hurt more than it did, but I actually felt relief."

He holds my gaze until I nod. "I can't say I'm surprised."

"I'm not either, she always was a selfish bitch."

I jerk back. "Whoa. I don't think I've ever heard you talk about her that way."

"I know I've been a mess lately and I haven't exactly talked about it with you, but I was a mess because I'm sad that Natalie will never know her mother. Not because of losing Johanna. Let me tell you, trying to make something work with the wrong person never goes well. No matter why you think you should try, sometimes it's better to just let them go."

"Uh huh." I finish my water and move to the floor to play with Natalie. "It's okay to feel sad for you too, you know."

Natalie brings me a book, so I start reading it to her until she takes it away from me and waddles off to her room. She's a busy child, constantly playing or talking.

"I'm serious. I was trying to make something work because of Nat, if it wasn't for her things would have ended way sooner. I'm ready to focus on Nat, and one day I will find someone truly worth my time."

"Let me get this straight, you had your heart ripped out and now you're going to risk it again?" I shake my head at him, resisting the urge to roll my eyes.

"Yes, because it's worth it. Loving unconditionally and without letting fear control us is the best thing we do. I don't want Natalie to grow up thinking love is scary." He watches

adoringly as she comes back into the kitchen still holding the book. "What I felt for Johanna wasn't real love, but when relationships end it still hurts, even when it's not right. But it's still worth it."

"It's not just scary, it's terrifying." We look on as she gathers her toys and moves them to a different room. I chuckle softly, she's such a weird kid, I love it.

"A piece of advice. If she comes along and doesn't terrify you a little, she's probably not the one for you, but if she scares the shit out of you, you push aside that fear and take a leap." Billy gets up, preheating the oven before removing a lasagna from the fridge. "All things worth our attention should be a little scary."

"How can you be so optimistic? You were a mess."

Billy sits across from me at the table, his face serious. "Carter, of course I was a mess. I had a baby with a woman I wasn't even certain I loved. Then to top it off, she leaves us. I didn't know what I was doing. I was tired and I needed to figure my shit out quickly. My job is making this work, but it's not easy. Single parenthood is tough, but I wouldn't change what Natalie and I have. We're better off and I know that. Now I'm free to make one hundred percent of the decisions."

"I didn't realize you felt that way. I thought—well, you know what I thought."

"CJ, you're twenty and need to focus on school. I wasn't about to put all of that on you. I didn't realize you were taking it so much to heart. We didn't have the most loving role model, but don't live your life like Dad. Love keeps us from being cold shells of a human being. It's worth the hurt."

cjtalks

Rumor has it that there is a pair of tickets for the Jasper Music Fest hidden somewhere on campus. Yes, I know Parkland is massive, but I can guarantee they're inside one of the academic buildings.

When you find them don't forget to tag me.

Have fun, and good luck.

#parklanduniversity #studentlife #cjtalks

CTJ2176: *So, I just found out my brother applied for a job in Vancouver. I saw him a couple of days ago and he didn't say anything, instead he tells me today over the phone. I'm fucking pissed.*

BNA3668: *That sucks...*

CTJ2176: *What?*

BNA3668: *What do you mean, what?*

CTJ2176: *You have a tone.*

BNA3668: *How can I have a tone? I'm typing.*

CTJ2176: *There is a tone. We've been chatting for weeks now, I can tell. Just say whatever it is that you're thinking.*

BNA3668: *Truth moment. I totally get why you would be upset, but maybe he just needs a fresh start. Someplace where he can create a new life. Haven't you ever wanted a change of scenery? Or a way to start over?*

CTJ2176: *I suppose...*

BNA3668: *I can understand where he is coming from. I've been tempted to leave here so I don't have to see Caterina's father all the time.*

CTJ2176: *Wait—Cat's father attends school here? And he doesn't bother asking about his kid?*

BNA3668: *Yeah. Although, I don't think he recognizes me.*

CTJ2176: *How is that even possible?*

BNA3668: I look drastically different than I did two years ago. Not that it's an excuse, but it's my reality. I need to keep my mouth shut, as much as it pains me, I need the child support. We barely make it by with it, I can't imagine how screwed we would be without it.

CTJ2176: I hate that you can't confront him.

BNA3668: Me too. Not that I want to confront him, but I want him to tell me to my face that he has no interest in being a father.

CTJ2176: How do you even receive child support if you never talk to him?

BNA3668: Through his father, who is not the warmest man in the world. In fact, he scares me and he knows it. I would say he even thrives on it.

CTJ2176: Now that I can relate to.

BNA3668: Where are those tickets hidden?

CTJ2176: I'm not telling you.

BNA3668: No one has been able to find them yet, and I desperately want to go.

CTJ2176: They haven't been hidden that long.

BNA3668: One clue.

CTJ2176: Okay, let's make a deal, the concert is mid-September and it's sold out. If I give you a clue and you find them, you take me.

BNA3668: . . .

BNA3668: . . .

BNA3668: Deal.

CTJ2176: They're tucked behind a sign, but the edges are sticking out.

BNA3668: That's a good clue.

CTJ2176: I want to meet you . . .

CARTER

I SIT ON the edge of my bed, resting my elbows on my knees, Billy's voice fading as my ears start ringing. The gray walls of my bedroom grow blurry as all the blood rushes from my head as I stand back up to pace the small space. Every muscle is tense, but I need to move.

"Carter? Are you even listening to me?" Billy shouts, startling me.

"Yeah, of course." I lie.

"I know it's a lot to process, but I think it's the best choice for me and Natalie. I hope you understand." His voice is firm, his mind made up.

I mumble a response. The job is an incredible opportunity, paying close to twice as much as he makes now, with a daycare right in the building. My brother is happier than I've ever heard him, and here I am wishing he wouldn't have gotten the job. I am possibly the worst brother in existence.

"It's an eight-hour drive. We're not moving across the country."

"I know, I know. I am happy for you, it's just—it sucks." Tilting my head back, I stare at the ceiling. "I guess it's time for you to move forward with your life, you are pretty damn old."

He laughs gruffly, putting Natalie on the phone to babble for a bit while he gets their dinner out of the oven. My heart aches

at the thought of seeing them less, but the idea of Billy trapping himself here in misery is worse than the temporary hole their leaving will cause.

I wander into the kitchen to grab a beer.

Billy comes back on the phone, giving me the details of the move. It's happening quickly, they want him there and ready to work in two weeks. We plan on seeing each other before he goes, but with packing, football, and him needing to find a place, I think we will only get one visit in. When we hang up, I leave my room and drop down on the couch, the scratchy pillow Jaden loves propping my head up.

Before I've even thought about what I'm doing, I'm sending Breanne a message.

> *CTJ2176:* Billy got the job. He and Natalie are moving.

> *BNA3668:* I'm happy for him, but I know how tough this must be on you.

> *CTJ2176:* Maybe I just need something to look forward to, keep my mind off it. Did you find those tickets yet?

> *BNA3668:* Do you realize how many posters, pictures, notices, bulletin boards, and other random crap there is hanging on these walls?

> CTJ2176: I do.

> *BNA3668:* Then you know the damn answer to that question.

CHAPTER 8

Nella

June

TAKING CATERINA'S HAND, I help her walk across the street to the park. Grace's neighborhood is well-established, many of the people living here empty-nesters. Most of the people in her apartment building are older couples, which I love. I love the friendly atmosphere and how much the other tenants care for Cat and Grace.

When Grace first moved in, halfway through my first semester of on-campus studies, they all welcomed her with casseroles, pies, lasagnas, and more food than she could possibly eat. It was like something from the movies.

Caterina stumbles a bit as she walks, her smile never leaving her face. I love that about children. They can stumble, hell even fall forward, and laugh it off. They hold nothing back because they don't know fear.

My biggest wish would be to shield her from hurt forever. I know that's not realistic, but I will do my best for as long as possible.

We get to the park, Cat plopping down into the sand without paying attention to anything else. I sit next to her, going along with whatever she does. Grabbing my phone, I take some pictures of her. She's growing so fast; I feel like every weekend when I come here she's different.

"Hey, birthday girl. I knew you would be here."

Looking up, I smile at Grace. "I would rather spend my birthday with you two than with anyone else."

We play at the park, Grace smiling each time I get a text from my friends wishing me a happy birthday. I know Ava wants to do something, but I'm resisting. Something tells me when I get home tonight there will be a reason for me to go by their apartment, but I can't stay here another night so there is no avoiding it.

By the time I tuck Caterina in, I'm dreading the drive back to campus. It's not that I don't enjoy my time there, but I hate leaving Cat. School doesn't hold the same appeal to me anymore. I refuse to drop out though, I need this for Cat, for our future.

"Drive safely, Nell." Grace gives me a tight hug, slipping a small box into my hands.

"What's this? We agreed no presents." I drop it into my purse, knowing arguing with her won't get me anywhere.

"It's just something small. Now get your butt back to campus so your friends can surprise you." She pushes me out the door.

Just as I thought, Ava is waiting outside my apartment when I get home. "You're finally home. Leave your stuff here, and let's go celebrate."

She drags me upstairs, pulling me into the apartment she shares with Dax and Peyton. As I was expecting, my friends are waiting with a cake and gifts.

"I told you not to make a big deal out of my birthday." I look around the small gathering. At least it's nothing compared to the other birthdays we've celebrated.

"Hush." Ava leads me to the couch, of course, I'm sitting next to Carter, and hands me a gift from her, Dax, and Peyton.

"I hate celebrating my birthday," I mumble, as I tear into the paper. Opening the box, I stare at the jacket inside. It's a dark gray coat made from this soft canvas type material. Perfect for the spring and fall. It's lined with checkered cotton, a purple and teal combination.

"I saw you eyeing it the other day when we went to the mall."

I hold it up, in complete shock that my friends would buy this for me. "It's too much."

"No, it's not." Ava doesn't comment on the torn state of my current jacket. She knows I'm attending Parkland on a full scholarship and that I can't afford to spend much money on myself. Whenever we go shopping, I never buy anything. Fingering the material, I feel a lump in my throat as I appreciate how wonderful my friends are, even though I still can't believe they bought this for me. It's a two-hundred-dollar jacket.

Setting it aside, I blink back the tears forming. "Wow. Thank you guys so much."

I move to get something to drink when Carter stops me and hands me another box. "You're not done." He smiles at me. I don't miss the nervous tilt to his lips, or the way he wipes the palms of his hands on his jeans.

I don't think I've ever seen Carter nervous. It piques my curiosity as to what could be in the box. It's significantly smaller than the one from Ava, Dax, and Peyton. I open it, unsure what to expect. As I fold back the tissue paper, I gasp. It's a silver necklace with a horseshoe charm.

I've been working for Lia for a couple of weeks now and I absolutely love it. Just last week I was telling my friends over dinner how much I'm learning and how incredible my boss is.

Lifting the necklace out of its box, I run my fingertips over the smooth, brushed silver. I've never been given a necklace before, not to mention the fact that he's paid close enough attention to know that a horseshoe would mean something to me.

Working with Lia has been so wonderful for me in every way, I feel more comfortable in my own skin as I learn from her and

the animals.

"I have no words. Thank you." I finally look up at Carter. I've been trying to meet his gaze more frequently instead of shying away. It's time to stop making myself small, find the courage of the girl who told him she wanted him rather than the woman who chooses to hide.

The nervous smile is gone, replaced by his usual cocky smirk. "It's not a big deal."

His phone dings with a text, and before Ava can serve the cake he's excusing himself. I look at the empty spot next to me longingly. This necklace is proof that the sweet guy I once knew still exists somewhere in there. It's too bad exposing myself to him would put everything I hold dear at risk.

It's not until I met Andie, and through her everyone in this room, that I began to feel like I found true friends. It's interesting how quickly friendships from high school dissolve. People move away, life circumstances change, and it's easy to lose touch. I don't feel like that will happen here. Even with everything I'm keeping from them, I know they won't sever our friendship because they're too loyal.

By the time I'm lying in bed, I have a content smile on my face. I run my fingers over my new necklace as I close my eyes. This is the best birthday I can remember having.

"Okay, now you want to stretch her neck out which will in turn stretch all those muscles I showed you on the chart, so pull the carrot away from her so she extends her neck for it." Lia watches as I follow her instructions. "Good. Now give her a carrot and pat her on the head. This tells her we're done and that she won't get any more treats."

I pat Belle on her forehead before taking her halter off.

"She likes you." I turn and see a stunning woman leaning against the fence watching us with a warm smile. "She doesn't usually take to strangers."

"Nella, this is my future sister-in-law and best friend, Emma." Lia introduces us. Emma swings over the fence and walks over to shake my hand. "It's nice to meet you. Lia has been raving about you since you started. I had to meet you."

I feel my face flush as I smile with pride. "I'm really enjoying myself. I've never been around horses before, but I love it. It's so—peaceful."

Emma's other mare, Serenity, comes up and nuzzles Emma's shoulder. We chat for a while before Lia and I head back to the clinic.

"How is your summer course going?" The trees loom over us as we walk. Their property is beautiful and massive. In the two weeks I've been working for Lia, she's taught me about the various aspects of their ranch and I'm growing to love it more each time. I hope I will have the chance to explore the rest of the property as well as meet the other members of her family and learn more about what they do.

"I'm almost done. I have two weeks left. Then I need to decide what I'm doing the rest of June, July, and August." We step into the clearing behind her clinic. The building still takes my breath away, it's massive and state of the art, yet still has a rustic appearance that fits with the ranch. "I think I might take July off to spend with Caterina."

"Who is Caterina?"

"My daughter. She is fifteen months old and lives with my sister in Hinton." I wait for the look of judgment to cross her face when I tell her Cat lives with Grace. I still remember the argument Grace and I got into when she told me she thought I should live on campus, get the full college experience. It was the worst one we've ever been in.

"You should bring her here one day," Lia suggests.

"You don't think that I'm a bad mom because she doesn't live with me?"

Lia frowns at my question, her lips tilting down as she reaches out to rest her hand on my arm. "Nella, you need to do what works for you. Emma's dad worked out of town Monday through Friday until she was six years old. That's basically what you're doing."

She drops her hand and leads us into her office. I shut the door to behind me, sighing at the cool air of the room. "That's what Grace says. And my friend, CJ, too."

"They both sound smart and you should listen to them. You may bring Grace along too, if you like." Lia grabs her clipboard, checking over our schedule for the day. "Everyone who works here is part of our family, that includes you and your family."

Smiling, I agree. It would be nice to bring them here to see this place. I don't know what led Ms. Waters to think of this, but I'm so grateful she did. In two weeks I've noticed my anxiety lessening, I remember what it feels like to have confidence in myself. It is astonishing to be doing something that I feel passionate about and that's making me look forward to my days so much more.

BNA3668: *Guess what.*

CTJ2176: *What?*

BNA3668: *That's not guessing.*

CTJ2176: *You murdered Cat's father and need help hiding the body?*

BNA3668: *Ha. Ha. Ha. No. I found the tickets!!*

CTJ2176: *Finally!*

BNA3668: *That's all you have to say? We at last have a date that we will meet, and you say finally?*

CTJ2176: *You have no idea how incredibly excited I am that I will get to meet you.*

BNA3668: *I just hope you're not disappointed with me in person.*

CTJ2176: *You're not the only one who has that fear.*

BNA3668: *You're scared you will be disappointed with me too?*

CTJ2176: *Hardy har har. Funny girl. You know I meant I'm worried you will be disappointed with me in person.*

BNA3668: *Not possible.*

CTJ2176: *How was your day?*

BNA3668: *Fantastic. Since I'm done with all the coursework for stats I stayed in Hinton with Grace and Caterina.*

CTJ2176: *What did the three of you do?*

BNA3668: *I sent Grace away for the weekend so she could have a break. She went to Edmonton to visit a friend of hers.*

CTJ2176: *That was nice of you.*

BNA3668: *She does so much for me, it's the least I can do. Cat and I went to the park every day. I bought her some new clothes, and we played in her ball pit.*

CTJ2176: *She has a ball pit???*

BNA3668: *Yeah, I bought a kiddie pool and filled it with these awesome balls I found on sale.*

CTJ2176: *Damn, that's cool.*

CHAPTER 9

CARTER

THE DOOR SLAMS into my back almost knocking the pizza and beer I'm carrying out of my hands. I hear something smack on the ground, and then the crown of Nella's hair fills my vision as she helps stabilize the pizza that is attempting to topple to the ground.

Once she's sure the pizza isn't going to fall, she turns to pick up the heaping laundry basket she abandoned in order to help me without a word.

Now that I'm not trying to save one hundred dollars' worth of pizza and beer, I look her over. Her dark hair is in a messy knot on top of her head, and she's wearing these awesome purple-rimmed glasses. Huh, I didn't know she wore glasses, but they look sexy as fuck on her.

As she straightens, those brown eyes the color of dark chocolate meet mine. That familiar feeling of knowing her from somewhere rises with unusual force. There is a tugging in my memory, but it's just out of reach. I know I know her from somewhere. I never thought I would be that guy. The guy to forget someone who obviously left an impact on me at some point. I hate not knowing where I recognize her from, because I clearly was around her for more than a moment.

"Guys night with Dax?" Her voice just reinforces the feeling, her tone not as quiet as usual. Ever since she started working at that horse place she seems to have more confidence. It just attracts me to her more.

She's not my usual type, but there is something about her that draws me in. There is a pull I've never felt before. No, that's a lie, I've felt it once before. Maybe it's because she's not the type of girl I usually hook up with. Despite how shy she is, it's obvious she's comfortable in her own skin, which is sexy. She typically wears comfortable, but sexy jeans and awesome graphic t-shirts, but she can pull off a sexy dress. Smiling when I think back to the first time I saw her, dressed in a sexy number I know Kensi forced her to wear. That night I couldn't get her out of my head. In fact, I haven't been able to get her out of my head every night since then.

She clears her throat, giving me a small smile. I've lost myself in my thoughts, thoughts of her, and just left her question hanging.

Nella's birthday was a turning point for us. She's been warmer towards me when we've seen each other, and I hope one day I can solve the mystery that surrounds her. For now, I'm happy that the weird awkwardness that always surrounded us is disappearing.

"Nah, I just thought I would bring a pizza by and see if they wanted to watch a movie. Why don't you join us?"

Nella shifts in place. "Umm."

"C'mon. It's Wednesday night, what better way to pass hump day?" I smirk when she blushes.

"Okay. Just let me change and I will see you all up there."

We part on the third floor, her tiny frame disappearing into her apartment. Once I get to Dax and Ava's apartment, I let myself in.

"I brought pizza and beer."

Dax and Ava look up from where they are cuddling on the couch. Seeing them reminds me what Billy said about love. I can admit that what he said is true. Being in love with Ava brought out the best in Dax. Same with Andie and Lucas. They are proof that when you find the right partner, your best self comes out. I see proof of it every day.

Setting everything on the counter, I open the boxes and grab a bunch of plates from the cupboard, handing Dax and Ava each one.

"Thanks, man. Babe, why don't you text Nella and see if she wants to come up. She probably has no food since she just got back from her sister's house yesterday." Dax takes out a few beers, handing me and Ava one.

"I ran into her in the hall, she's on her way up—I didn't realize she was away."

"Yeah, she goes to her sister's house in Hinton every Friday night, usually she comes home on Sunday's but this weekend she extended her stay."

Opening my beer, I tilt it back. The cool, hoppy taste fills my mouth as I think about this new information. "I didn't realize her sister lives in Hinton."

Before Dax can respond, Nella comes inside. She's changed out of her sweats into a pair of jeans and her glasses are gone. While she still looks sexy, I'm disappointed she felt like she had to change her clothes rather than be cozy.

We help ourselves to pizza while searching Netflix for something to watch. In the end, we settle on marathoning *Orange is the New Black*. If I'm being honest with myself, I'm not paying attention, and by the third episode I am totally lost as to what's happening. I could not give one detail about this show if someone asked me.

I've been distracted all day. My cell has been eerily silent today, after talking with Breanne throughout most of the day for a couple of weeks now, I'm feeling the withdrawal.

Then when she told me she found the tickets and knowing I

get to meet her in September, I felt an elation I only recall experiencing once. On the night I slept with Breanne Cooper.

Waking up next to her was so surreal. I was looking forward to seeing her smile when I woke her up, but then my father called demanding I come home immediately.

Talk about a splash of ice cold water.

My biggest regret is that I didn't tell him to go to hell and stay, instead I hightailed it out of there leaving her alone. I've searched for her on Facebook, Instagram, Tumblr, and Twitter. My Breanne Cooper is nowhere to be found. Somehow I need to forgive myself for it and hope she is happy wherever she is.

I don't want to have a regret that will top that by never meeting this Breanne in person and seeing if the connection I feel with her carries on in person.

Nella accidentally elbows me as she sets her plate down, startling me from my thoughts. Her eyes flash up to me as she apologizes. Her cheeks flushing pink when I wink at her.

She drops her gaze, a small smile on her lips as she arranges the pizza on her plate. I've been drawn to her from the first time I saw her, but how long can I hold out waiting to see if she ever warms up to me. Not that I've put much of an effort in. I can admit that over the past eight months I probably did everything I could to deter myself and her from getting too close. But I need to consider the attraction between us, because I know it's not one-sided.

I'm just tired. I'm tired of not being myself. I'm exhausted of fighting feelings that are stronger than I am.

Feelings that have put me into a tricky situation simply because I have fought them for so long. One girl I've never met in person, the other I can hardly get to tolerate my presence. How am I supposed to choose when there is no clear answer?

Nella's phone rings, loud in the quiet room. She glances at the screen, a real, full-blown smile filling her face. It's stunning and I can't stop looking at the way her eyes have lit up. "It's my sister, I need to get this."

Ava pauses the show as Nella stands and answers her phone.

"Where is Peyton tonight?" I ask as I watch Nella talk. She's still smiling, her words muffled as Ava tells me that Peyton went to see her brother. I mumble something appropriate as I watch Nella straighten a photo on the wall.

"Grace . . ." That one name drowns out every other sound in the room. Leaning forward, I listen carefully as I try to hear what she's saying. Dax and Ava go into the kitchen to get new drinks, making it easier for me to eavesdrop since Nella is speaking so quietly. I can barely make out what she's saying.

I'm in the midst of trying to figure out how to hear her better when she paces back across the room bringing her closer to me.

"Seriously, stop." Nella peeks at me out of the corner of her eye, before angling away from me. "You do so much for me. Grace, I'm serious."

She listens for a while, smiling softly. "I love you too."

She hangs up, settling back onto the couch. I'm frozen in place as she picks up her pizza once again and starts munching. Her posture is relaxed, completely unaware of the turmoil occurring in my head right now.

Her sister's name is Grace? My gut screams at me as I finally put things together, many small things in typed conversations begin to stand out. There have been several similar coincidences that I've ignored. The similar schedules. The extended weekend with a sister in Hinton. And now their sister has the same name? Is it possible that Nella and Bre are the same person?

Typing in my passcode, I select the Parkland Chat app on my cell and send Breanne a quick message.

CTJ2176: You've been quiet today.

Nella's phone chimes.

She glances at the screen and smiles the biggest smile I've ever seen on her face, bigger than the one when she was talking to her sister. My heart thuds heavily in my chest as she types quickly before setting her phone face up on the armrest of the loveseat.

My cell buzzes.

BNA3668: Sorry. I had to drive home and then did a ton of laundry. My friends and I are watching Netflix and eating pizza right now.

Holy. Shit. Nella is Breanne. Breanne is *Nella.*

Well, I guess that solves one of my problems. The two women I can't get out of my head are one and the same. I can't believe how many signs I've missed or ignored. This changes so much.

Dax and Ava come back in, handing Nella and me fresh beers. They start the show up again, but I'm no longer pretending to watch. Nella keeps glancing at her phone, chewing on her lower lip as she waits for my response.

CTJ2176: I hope I'm not bothering you.

BNA3668: Not at all. It's kind of an awkward evening anyways.

CTJ2176: Why?

BNA3668: Well two of my friends make one of the cutest couples ever, and the only other person here is that guy I told you about. So, it's just this weird non-double date and to top it off I always feel a little on guard.

Wracking my brain, I try to think of everything Bre—Nella— has said about her friends. I remember her saying one of the guys and her have a weird history, but that can't be me. Unless—she did say he didn't remember her and I do recognize her from somewhere, but from where?

I'm slowly processing this revelation. Connecting everything I know about Breanne with Nella. Holy crap, Nella has a kid. And she apparently knows me from somewhere.

CTJ2176: Oh, right, that guy.

By the time we call it a night, all I can think about is tossing a football and working this out in my head. I can't believe I didn't realize it until now.

Why did she say her name is Breanne? At least now I won't get confused over my two Breanne's anymore.

As I walk to my apartment my head clears enough that I finally realize how much knowing this information can help me win Nella over. I know it's wrong, but it's better to ask forgiveness—right?

cjtalks

#randomthoughtfriday

I always thought I had everything figured out. Get my degree in Sports Med. Move on to my masters. Move far away from my jerk of a father. Eventually find someone and settle down. Then I started attending Parkland. I've finished my second year, and I realize I don't have shit figured out.

The person people see walking around is only a small part of who I am. And why? Because it's easier to be who they think I am. I'm even deceiving my friends. They don't know I have this blog. The person they think they know is just a persona, sure that persona has attributes that are me, but it's all surface.

It sucks living with a secret. It sucks feeling like you can't be yourself.

I don't really have a point to this blog post. I guess I just want everyone who feels lost to know they're not alone. Even the most together looking person has doubts.

#parklanduniversity #studentlife #cjtalks

CTJ2176: *Have a good weekend with Caterina.*

BNA3668: *I can't go. My car has a flat, and whomever tightened the nuts on the rim made them too tight for me.*

The **NO JOCK** *Rule*

CTJ2176: *I'm so sorry.*

BNA3668: *It's okay. I will clean the apartment and ask one of my friends to help me out tomorrow.*

CHAPTER 10

Nella

I'M PRONE ON the couch, tears running down my face when someone knocks on the door. I consider ignoring it, but decide to see who it is. Swiping away the tears with my sleeve, I open the door to find Carter on the other side.

"What are you doing here?" My voice is hoarse from sobbing, but I'm too upset to care that he's seeing me like this.

"I noticed you had a flat tire, I came to get your keys so I can change it." I gape at him, frozen in place. He looks over my shoulder and notices my keys hanging halfway out of my purse. Without a word, he reaches around me and takes them before strutting away leaving me staring at an empty doorway.

When I finally gather my wits about me, I snatch up my purse and duffle bag. Locking the bottom lock, I race down the stairs and to my car. Carter already has the wheel off and is tightening the spare tire into place.

He shuts everything into the trunk, including my bag, and hands me my keys.

My face feels scratchy from crying, my eyes are puffy, and my contacts itch, but in that moment, none of it matters. I walk over to Carter and wrap my arms around his waist. The top of my

head brushes against his chin as I rest my cheek on his hard chest. His arms encircle me, holding me to him. It feels so right, I could stay in this place for hours.

"Thank you so much." The words are a whisper, but I know that he can hear me.

Stepping back, I tuck a strand of hair behind my ear and smile up at him. Carter loops his thumbs into his pocket, dropping his chin as he looks down at me. "Go, enjoy your weekend."

BNA3668: *That final was brutal. I'm sure I passed, but I've never been so nervous watching the hands on a clock move.*

CTJ2176: *I know. I'm not sure I passed.*

BNA3668: *I'm sure you did. A girl next to me was writing a biology final, I thought she was going to start crying. I felt so bad.*

CTJ2176: *The guy next to me was also writing stats, he got up within an hour. I'm sure he just gave up.*

BNA3668: *Now that you're free, are you heading anywhere for the rest of summer vacation?*

CTJ2176: *No. Billy is in Vancouver, so there is nowhere else for me to go. Plus, with work, it's just easier to stay here.*

BNA3668: *Are you ever going to stop evading me when I ask you where you work?*

CTJ2176: *I don't want to tell you.*

BNA3668: Why?

CTJ2176: *Because of something you said a couple weeks ago.*

BNA3668: *Just tell me! Unless you're ashamed. Are you a stripper? A gigolo? A circus clown?*

CTJ2176: You're insane. Do your friends know just how crazy you are?

BNA3668: No . . . I'm much more subdued around them. And you're avoiding the question.

CTJ2176: Fine. It's not really a job job, I have football camp. I just know you're not fond of jocks because of Cal's dad. And I liked that you knew me as someone other than a football player. No one else sees me the way you do. Plus, I'm thinking of quitting, I just don't enjoy it as much as I used to.

. . . You should show your friends the side of you I get to see.

CTJ2176: Bre?

BNA3668: I'm here. Just thinking.

CTJ2176: That's not good.

BNA3668: I was just thinking that maybe it's time for me to let that go. Besides, I think you're awesome, even if you are a jock. Plus, hello kettle, you're black. Why don't you show your friends this side of you?

CTJ2176: You're right. Maybe someday.

"Grace, I don't know what to do." I jump up onto the counter after tucking Caterina in. Grace is putting the finishing touches on her delicious homemade brownies. My mouth waters as she sticks the pan in the oven.

"What do you mean?" She leans against the counter, handing me the mixing spoon.

I take it reverently, eating the delicious chocolatey batter before continuing. "Ever since he fixed my tire, Carter has been showing up randomly and doing nice things for me. First the tire. Then a day after my coffee pot breaks he's at my door with a steaming double-double. And here I am keeping the worst kind of secret from him."

"Nell, it's not that cut and dry." She takes the now clean spoon and sticks it in the dishwasher. "I wonder why he's being all sweet."

"He's never been rude to me. I've never given him the opportunity to be nice before. I guess I'm tired of hiding. He clearly doesn't recognize me, so why not allow myself to enjoy being close to him?"

"I still don't get it." She looks me over. "I guess you do look different, I just can't imagine not recognizing someone I knew only two years ago."

"You didn't recognize the guy you went out with last year when we ran into him at the grocery store today." I point out.

"That's different, I blocked that disaster out."

"Well, maybe he blocked me out."

She frowns at me. The timer on the oven dings, freeing me from her displeasure. I'm not wrong, he could have. I was no one. Kind of frumpy and awkward. I'm one of those women who didn't blossom until after high school.

"Anyway, I think I'm going to embrace the fact he doesn't recognize me and maybe he can get to know me as I am now."

"Just be careful. When you look at Caterina you can see the similarities. One day you're going to have to tell your friends about this aspect of your life." Grace cuts the pan of brownies in half, one for each of us.

I take my plate and settle onto the couch. "I hate this stupid contract hanging over my head, but I guess that doesn't mean I can't tell them about her."

Grace sits next to me, tucking her knees up to her chest. "Has Marshall gotten back to you about renegotiating the contract?"

I shake my head. She sighs, placing her hand on my shoulder and squeezing. "You have a lot of thinking to do."

"I know."

She starts the movie, both of us eating our brownie in silence.

If I was to sit down with someone and tell them about my

life, they would think I was making it up, but I can't make this shit up. Grace is right, I do have thinking to do.

I have been in love with Carter since I was sixteen years old. Carter asked me to dance when he overheard some girls making fun of me. Despite his good looks, he never hung out with the mean crowd, he just got along with everyone.

Maybe it's time to let go of the fact he left me that one night. Maybe he saved me from an awkward morning after. I've spent so many years being angry at him because he not only left me but chose to ignore his child, but can I fault him for something he chose to do when he was eighteen? Haven't we all made mistakes?

It's time to start making changes and it starts with being honest with my friends. Opening our group text, I just start typing.

Me: It sucks that I'm doing this over text, but I can't keep this in anymore.

Kensi: Are you okay?

Me: I am, it's just I haven't been completely honest about my life.

Andie: Should we sit down?

Ava: You know we love you, no matter what.

Peyton: Girl, there is nothing you could tell me that will shock me.

Me: When I was 18 I slept with my high school crush at a party. We were both drunk and in the morning, I woke up alone. It broke my heart. A month later I found out I was pregnant. The reason I go to my sister's every weekend is because she looks after my daughter. Caterina is fifteen months.

Ava: Why didn't you tell us?

Me: There is more to the story, I'm not ready to tell

you the rest yet.

Andie: What about the father?

Me: I signed a contract that states I'm not allowed to contact him in regards to Cat. In return, I make two grand a month in child support. It's barely enough to keep Grace and Cat afloat, but it's something.

Peyton: Holy. Shit.

Ava: You know we're here for you.

Kensi: I wish I was there to hug you.

Me: Less than a week and you will be. I'm so sorry I didn't tell you.

Andie: Girl, we all have secrets. It's no big deal. Girl's night when we get home.

Me: Please don't tell the guys, I'm not ready for them to know yet.

CTJ2176: How's your weekend going?

BNA3668: Good. I hate that I need to leave tomorrow morning. I don't know if I can do another two years of this.

CTJ2176: You're thinking of quitting school?

BNA3668: No, I need to figure out a career for myself. I'm thinking about moving to Hinton and commuting to school, though.

CARTER
July

"DUDE, YOU HAVE no idea how glad I am that you're back." Smacking Lucas on the back, I pick up the X-Box controller and load a new game. The girls are out for a girls' night, so we thought a game night was in order.

"It was an awesome trip, but I'm glad we're back. What's new?"

"Not much. Football camp is taking up a lot of my time. Coach Leblanc is pushing us pretty hard." My fingers fly over the buttons as we play. I'm still not enjoying myself, and it is showing. Coach pulled me aside the other day to call me out on my lack of enthusiasm. I know I will be sitting on the bench this season if I don't put on a better game face. I'm not sure I care.

"Nothing else?"

"Nah, not really."

Dax sits on the floor, his expression intent on the game. "Carter and Nella have been chatting online since the beginning of May. Nella has no idea she's talking to Carter."

I gape at him. He's so casual in the dropping of that bomb. "How did you know?"

He pauses and turns to me. "I saw your paper when I was at your place, and overheard Nella talking to Ava about the same topic. I put it together when Nella mentioned her partner CJ. Carter Jacobs, CJ, it's not the most difficult connection to make."

Lucas drapes an arm over the back of the couch, game forgotten. "Well, well, well. Are you finally going to do something about your attraction?"

I shrug. "Yeah. I guess what you guys have isn't so bad."

They laugh, restarting the game. "You're an idiot."

When she told me she's considering moving to Hinton, I saw the expiration date on my chances with her. I must move more quickly than I initially thought I would need to and that scares the shit out of me. Moving fast isn't something I think will work on Nella. I need to come up with a plan, but now is not the time.

For tonight, I'm just glad to have my crew back. Jaden returns home in a week and I need his insight. He's the only one I will tell the whole story to, he's a vault when it comes to information.

And rumor has it that Dean will be coming back soon. No one has heard from him since his brother passed away, aside from an occasional text letting us know he is planning on coming back.

It will be good to have everyone together in a room again.

The girls come in laughing as we wrap up our third game. Andie crawls onto Lucas' lap, while Ava curls into Dax. I look at what they have with each other with new eyes. I've been looking at relationships differently since my talk with Billy. Now I see them paired together and envy the closeness. I envy the fact they have someone who loves every part of who they are.

"Tell us about your vacation," Ava says, drawing my attention away from Nella.

We listen as Andie fills us in on everything they did. Hiking, boat tours, biking, paint ball, shopping, and all the craziness of Kensi's family.

As everyone laughs, I message Nella.

CTJ2176: Did you have a good girls' night?

Watching her pull her phone out, I see her smile as she replies. I wait a few minutes and take out my phone to read her message.

BNA3668: Yeah, we talked more about Cat since we were in person rather than on text. And we talked boys. Always a good time.

CTJ2176: How did they take the news about Cat?

Again, I slip my phone back inside my pocket. I watch once more as Nella smirks when she sees a text from me on her phone and types a response. Giving myself another couple of minutes to surreptitiously check my phone, I'm happy to see her take on sharing the news with our friends.

BNA3668: They were so supportive. My one girlfriend has a five-year-old son. He's on vacation with his dad until mid-August, but when he gets back we're going to set up a playdate.

CTJ2176: Sounds like you have awesome friends.

I sneak one last peek at my screen when I feel the message notification vibration.

BNA3668: I do. A few of them just got back from a two-month road trip, I'm so glad they're back.

Dax catches my eye, grinning at me as I put my phone away. I shake my head at him, narrowing my eyes in warning. He just grins wider as he glances towards Lucas.

What jackasses.

By the time one in the morning rolls around I'm yawning. Standing, "I'm going to head home."

"Me too." Nella follows me to the door. Our friends all wave, while not so subtly watching us. As we shut the door, she laughs softly to herself.

"What?" I chuckle too, because I'm sure I know why she's laughing.

"It's nothing, they're just funny."

"And we missed their crazy asses."

She nods, still smiling. Nella pauses on her landing, flushing a little when I press my hand into the small of her back and walk her to her door.

She unlocks the door and then turns to face me. "Well, I need to be at work in seven hours."

"Yeah, okay."

"Goodnight, Carter."

"Goodnight, Nella."

cjtalks

I want to thank everyone for the influx of messages I've received regarding my last blog post. I know it's been a while since I posted, but I want you to know how much I appreciate the support.

Recent updates re: Parkland hacks

Parkland will be hosting a writing contest for students. Two students will win a $1000 gift certificate for the bookstore. Second prize is $500 for one student. Third prize is $250 for one student. The submission deadline is July 15.

Don't miss out on Cinema in the Park this Sunday. There has been a load of suggestions and we're trying to work through them. This Sunday will feature *The Fault in Our Stars*.

Lastly, the summer session begins July 9. Last chance to withdraw from classes is July 25.

#parklanduniversity #studentlife #cjtalks

CTJ2176: Are you entering the contest?

BNA3668: *No, I qualified for a full scholarship for this upcoming semester. It wouldn't be fair to someone who needs the help.*

CTJ2176: *You're such an incredible person.*

BNA3668: *It shouldn't be a surprise for someone not to take something away from someone who could use it.*

CTJ2176: *You have more faith in people than I do.*

Knocking on Nella and Kensi's door, I balance the tray of coffee I'm holding on top of a box of muffins.

Kensi opens the door, smirking when she sees me. "Well, hello there."

"Is Nella around?"

She nods, stepping back so I can enter the apartment. Nella appears from down the hall, glasses perched on her nose, dark hair tumbling around her shoulders. Her eyes widen when she sees me, her hands flying to quickly zip up her hoodie, but not before I catch a glimpse of a sexy black camisole. Ignoring the way my body reacts; I wait for her to say something.

"What are you doing here?"

I don't have a reason, so I go with the truth. "I wanted to see you."

"Oh."

We stare at each other for so long that by the time I break away, Kensi has disappeared into her room.

Toeing off my shoes, I follow Nella further into her apartment, joining her on the couch. Awkwardness descending as we sip the coffee I brought.

Nella looks up at me, and starts to laugh.

"What?"

"This is just really awkward." She giggles again, and this time I join her.

"We've never really spent any time alone together. You always avoid me."

"I do not."

Cocking my head, I give her a pointed look. "C'mon."

"Okay, you're right."

"Want to tell me why?"

She grabs a muffin and starts pulling chunks out of it and popping them in her mouth. It's tough not to say anything, push her to be up front. I know there is a reason, she's said we have a tricky history when talking to me as CJ, but despite my prodding she's never told me why.

"It's not important." She looks up at me and smiles. A real smile. A smile that is so familiar to me I can feel that the memory is there, but the person it's attached to still evades me.

"I have a crazy question for you."

She tenses, setting her half-eaten muffin onto the coffee table. "What is it?"

"Ever since we met, I've felt like I know you from somewhere, but I can't put my finger on it." I watch her carefully for any changes in expression.

Her eyes flick away from me, her teeth gnawing on her lower lip.

"I used to live in the apartment underneath yours," she finally says.

"Hmmm, that must be it." I let it pass, despite knowing that's not it. I remember seeing her in the hall, she avoided me then too. Letting it go, I change the subject. "How's work going?"

"Really good. I actually need to be there in an hour."

"I guess I better go then."

She walks me to the door, her hands wrapped around her coffee. "Thank you for the coffee and muffins."

CHAPTER 12

Nella

"WHY DIDN'T YOU tell him?" Lia asks as she holds the door to the arena open for me.

I lead Ollie in for our morning riding lesson. "Because I'm a coward. Because I didn't want him to hightail it in the other direction. Because by telling him, I'm risking my ability to care for my daughter. The list goes on and on."

Lia watches as I mount Ollie and start moving him through his warmup. "I have some news."

She walks to the center of the arena, instructing me as I ride until she's satisfied with what I'm doing.

"What's going on?" My eyes are on where I'm going, my mind on my core and my legs and my hands.

"I'm pregnant."

"What? That's amazing!" I stop Ollie and turn towards her.

She's smiling, her hand rubbing circles on her still flat belly. "We're excited. It got me thinking though, how would you feel about training with me full-time in August? You have a natural talent and I've been talking about hiring someone for a while now. Plus, I'm going to need someone to start easing the workload and I adore having you here. I know you've said you're

83

set on finishing school. I've talked it over with Dane and Ryan and I can pay you a decent salary. There's an empty farmhand house for you, Cat, and Grace that would be included in your benefits package, which would start immediately."

My heart starts racing with excitement. The idea of working here full-time, living here too, is incredible. "I would love to. Would it be okay if we start with August and see if I can even do it? I would like to talk to Grace and think about the rest. Giving up school is a big step."

"Of course, I expected you to take time to think about it, you're not a rash person. If you decide it's what you want, we will sit down and hash out the details. Something you could consider is attending school part-time. We could go over the course calendar together to see if there is anything that you could use here. No pressure, though."

That night I'm on the phone with Grace, trying to work out what I want. "Can you imagine? We would have a rent-free house. I would have a salary. Doing a job I love."

"That's so wonderful, Nell." I can hear Grace's smile over the phone. "I'm proud of you for not committing without seeing if it works, but from what you say, big changes are in your future."

We chat a while longer before hanging up. When I turn around, I see Kensi standing in the middle of the living room, her face in a frown.

"Are you dropping out?"

"No. Well, I haven't decided anything."

"I don't want to lose you."

"Kens, regardless of whether I decide to work for Lia full time, you will never lose me." I walk over and hug her. "I'm just taking it day by day."

"I'm being selfish. I love living with you, although from what I overheard it's an incredible opportunity. Now, when do we get to meet Caterina?"

On our girls' night, I explained about the contract and told my friends that Cat's dad attends school here. I didn't tell them that Carter is her dad, but I know that as soon as they see her they will know. Her eyes, her face, everything but her hair comes from him.

"I don't know."

"C'mon, you know we all love kids. Why don't you bring her here one weekend? Or week?" Kensi pushes.

I smile. "We will see."

She grumbles to herself. I wish that our situation wasn't so complicated. I wish I could bring Cat here and not worry about breaching a contract. I wish I had the money in the bank so I could break the contract without worrying about what it would cost me, but that's not my reality.

I'm not angry with Carter anymore, but I wish I could confront him. He wants to know where he recognizes me from, but telling him isn't that simple.

Marshall still hasn't called me back. I've sent him several emails, no response. He's always been tough to get in contact with, but this screams avoidance. He's such an ass.

I go to my room and crawl into bed. I'm exhausted, but I toss and turn as I try to figure out a way to get everything out in the open without completely fucking Cat and me over.

I don't want to run away from Carter anymore. I don't want to hang on to these secrets. I don't want to go another day without seeing Caterina.

I need to make some decisions, and I don't even know where to start.

BNA3668: I hate being an adult.

CTJ2176: What's wrong?

BNA3668: I suck at making decisions. Lia offered me a full-time job and a rent-free place to live. I could see Caterina every day. I could save money and not rely on anyone else to care for my child.

CTJ2176: Wow. Is that what you want?

BNA3668: I don't know. I think so. I told her we would see how August goes. I'm working for her full-time as a trial.

CTJ2176: Have you talked to your friends about it?

BNA3668: My roommate. I'm sure the grapevine will hear about it soon enough.

"You're dropping out?" Andie, Peyton, and Ava corner me in the living room as soon as I walk in. I feel every set of eyes on me as I look at Kensi over Ava's shoulder. She avoids my gaze, busying herself with her phone.

"Nothing is decided."

I try to calm my friends down, assuring them if I take it we will still see each other. When I explain exactly what Lia offered, I know they understand why it would appeal to me.

"We get it. It's just so weird to think of you not being here."

"I'm already at my sister's every weekend. It's not that much different."

Ava comes to stand beside me, wrapping her arm around my waist. She gives Andie, Peyton, and Kensi the "mom" look. She understands better than anyone why I'm making this decision.

"It's just . . ." Andie starts.

"Guys, obviously Nella is putting a lot of thought into this. As her friends, shouldn't you support her decision to do what's best for her?" Carter snaps. The muscles in his jaw flex when he clenches his teeth, his eyes narrow on all of them in warning.

Every pair of eyes turns to look at him in surprise. Gulping when he looks straight at me, I hold his gaze fighting my initial instinct to look away. This is the Carter I remember from high school. The protective Carter. The one who stands up for people, no matter who they are.

We stare at each other until Dax clears his throat with a chuckle. "Dean just called, he should be here in five with Chinese for dinner."

The moment passes as we start gathering plates, cutlery, and drinks. When Carter passes me I put my hand on his arm to stop him.

Looking up, I gently squeeze his forearm and whisper, "Thank you."

His blue eyes search my face, now I know he's trying to figure out why he recognizes me. The urge rises to tell him, to see how he reacts, but even if I was going to I couldn't do it here, not with all our friends here to witness it.

"Nella, you need to do what's best for you. Besides, it's obvious you love working for Lia and since you've had this job you've come out of your shell more. I, for one, appreciate that, even if we will all miss having you around." He walks away, my hand trailing down his arm until it falls to my side, my fingertips tingling.

Curling my fingers into my palm, I paste on a smile as Dean comes in with food. He's spent most of the summer at his parents' house, the loss of his brother a devastating blow to the family. He has dark shadows under his eyes and his smile isn't quite as bright as it used to be, but he seems happy to be back.

The rest of the night I find myself watching Carter more than usual. Working with the horses and continuing to see Ms. Waters has helped me start to lose some of my anxiety, I feel more confident and, despite the risk, tonight has made me realize Carter deserves to know who I am.

Maybe once he finally has that clarification he will take the steps to rectify his choice regarding Caterina. I don't know how we could proceed otherwise and since Marshall refuses to respond this might be a way around my contractual silence.

CARTER

THE GUYS ARE over and gossiping like a bunch of women. I can't help but roll my eyes when Lucas fills us in on Kensi's antics while they were gone. We all know she likes men she has no future with so the stories aren't new to us.

It's all fun and games until Dax fills them in on my situation with Nella. He even called it a "situation."

Opening the door, I shoo them into the hall so we can hit the road. Our plans were to go paintballing, not to sit around gossiping.

"Can we just go paintballing?" I plead. It's not like I don't have guilt over using her relationship with CJ to get her to trust me, I'm not a complete asshole.

"So let me get this straight. You befriended Nella through Parkland Chat because you were paired together for a project, under the guise that her name is Breanne, but then discovered she was Nella? And you haven't told her you're the CJ she's been trusting with all sorts of personal information?" Lucas falls into step beside me as we head down the stairs, his eyes narrowing. "You better own up to that shit and soon. That's not something you withhold from someone and it's been going on long enough."

"You think I—" Freezing as I round the corner and see Nella halfway up the first flight of steps. I don't think I will ever forget the look of betrayal she shoots in my direction. "Nella."

Her voice is quiet when she cuts me off. "I've seen a lot of sides to you Carter, but this one—this one hits an all new low. I've forgiven you for a lot of shit, but I don't know if I can let this one go."

She turns to leave, stopping when I move to follow her. "Nella, I don't know what—if we could talk about what you mean maybe—please let me explain."

Without looking at me she walks to the door and opens it. "No." She pauses and finally looks up at me, her dark brown eyes practically snapping with anger. "At least, not right now." The door shuts with a resounding click. It's worse than if she would have slammed it and stormed off.

The five of us stand there in silence as we watch her walk away with her head held high.

"What the fuck?" Dean finally turns to me.

I don't know where to begin. There are things Nella told me that I will never betray, but these guys are my brothers and they deserve to know as much as I can tell them since I've just fucked up our little circle of friends.

Abandoning our paintball plans, we head back to the apartment. As we sit there, I explain how I know Nella from somewhere, but I can't pinpoint where. It's a feeling I've felt since I first saw her and when I asked she denied it, but in her anger, she must have forgot to keep playing that card.

"It's frustrating as hell. How can I not figure out who she is?"

"Why would she tell you her name is Breanne?"

"I have no idea. All I know is I need to talk to her. I need to make this right. I'm an asshole a lot of the time, but I told myself I wouldn't become my father and hurt everyone in order to help myself." Jaden comes into the room with a case of beer. Grabbing one, I crack the top and take a deep pull. "This is why I stick to one-night stands. No chance of involving emotions."

Dax looks at me like I'm stupid. "You're an idiot. I thought you were over that crap."

Rolling my head, I crack my neck. He's calling my bluff and he knows it. Nella isn't like Johanna, or like the gold-digging bitches my dad has brought home since my mom passed away.

She's sweet and honest and genuine. I don't think Nella is capable of betraying anyone.

The next morning I'm in the midst of a brutal football practice. Coach is in a foul mood and my lack of focus is making things worse for my entire team. I can't bring myself to care too much, the physical torture is better than the mental torture at trying to figure out how I can fix things with Nella.

I don't waste time after practice with showering or changing. A quick stop at the Starbucks and soon I'm standing outside Nella and Kensi's apartment, covered in dirt and grass, with a coffee peace offering. Knocking on the door, it doesn't surprise me when Kensi opens the door with a scowl on her face.

"You should just turn around and leave right now." She steps out into the hallway, closing the door behind her.

"Kensi, please just see if she will talk to me." I hold out the tray of coffee.

She just looks at it and then me in disgust. "Do you have any idea how much Nella needed a friend like CJ? Of course you do, because you were him and she opened up to you in a way she's never opened up to any of us."

"I didn't know until we'd already established the friendship. I should have told her and I didn't, it was wrong, but let me clear the air."

"She's not here. She's with Grace and Caterina."

"Do you—" She's already shaking her head.

"No, I don't." With that, Kensi turns from me and goes back into her apartment. Her hand squeezes the door before she turns back around. "She needs to process this, give her a chance to work through it and I'm sure she will come to you."

Leaving their building, I walk to a nearby bench and pull out my phone. Opening the Parkland Chat app, I ignore Kensi's suggestion to give her time. This is the only way I know I will reach Nella, even if she doesn't respond, I need to try.

CTJ2176: Nella, please talk to me.

CTJ2176: I know I messed up, but I would like a chance to explain, in person.

cjtalks

#confession

I recently hurt someone that is more important to me than I ever anticipated and while I understand why she is not speaking to me, I hope that she reads this and gives me a chance to make things right.

Something I've never told anyone, not even my brother, is that I have attachment issues. At least that's what a counselor I saw all throughout junior high told me and my father. My father, who is someone I have little to no respect for, brushed it off and told me it's called being strong. The thing I've come to realize, especially as of late, is that it takes more strength to let someone in that to keep them out. I was doing that with "Breanne," a woman I met via Parkland Chat who didn't know my true identity. To be fair, in the beginning I didn't know who she was either. We talked about things we couldn't share with others, both for our own reasons.

Let's back up a little and I will explain what exactly my Attachment Disorder looks like, because it's different for everyone. I am capable of trusting and attaching to people, but for self-preservation reasons I choose not to, especially women. I choose to keep most people at a distance, and when they don't want to tolerate it anymore, I let them go without a second thought.

My mother died when I was very young, and the types of women my father brought home had no interest in me or my brother. So here I am, twenty years old, and the only relationships I have under my belt are a series of one night stands, which aren't actual relationships. Of all of those, there is only one I regret because she was special to me. But I'm getting off topic.

In May, I met "Breanne" and maybe it was her name and the association I have with another Breanne I once knew, but we became friends and talked to each other. Not too long ago, I found out "Breanne's" true identity is someone within my close circle of friends. Rather than telling her, I used my connection to get closer to her.

Like most secrets, I was exposed and here we are. Now the rest of our circle of friends will know the person behind this blog, something I never intended, but for this purpose I've made peace with it.

Breanne, I hope you read this and that you reach out to me. I made a mistake and for the first time rather than cutting my losses, I want to make it right. I'm scared as hell over what could be, but I would rather know than live a life of wondering.

#parklanduniversity #studentlife #cjtalks

CHAPTER 14

Nella

"MA, MA. UP." Cat holds her arms up giving me a toothy grin. I bend and pick her up, blowing a raspberry on her belly.

Balancing her on my hip when my cell rings, I smile when I see it's Kensi. "Hey. It's a little early for you to be up, isn't it?"

"I'm trying something new. It sucks and I don't want to talk about it." She laughs, but it's the most awkward laugh I've heard come out of Kensi.

"Are you okay?"

"Fine. I just thought I should let you know Carter came by last night with coffee in the hopes of talking to you. I told him to go away, but you may want to check out that blog—cjtalks."

"Do I actually want to?" Caterina giggles as I blow a raspberry on her cheek before setting her back down. She wanders off to her toy corner and starts playing.

"Yes. Was that Cat? Why won't you let me meet her?" I hear the fridge open in the background, a loud gulping sound soon following.

"One day you will meet her, and that day you will know why."

"So cryptic," she teases.

We hang up after I let her know I won't be home until after work tomorrow. Locking myself in the bathroom, I sit on the edge of the tub and open Tumblr. Holding my breath, I search for Carter's blog and start reading his latest post.

Air comes in and out of me in gasps, and I'm rereading his blog post for the third time when Grace finally pokes her head in the door.

"Nell? Are you having a panic attack?" She comes in, shutting the door behind her.

"Cat?"

"She's playing." Grace takes my phone from me, setting it on the counter as she pushes my head between my knees. Closing my eyes, I breathe in deeply.

"I'm not having a panic attack." Pushing her hands out of the way, I grab my phone, scroll to the top of the post and hand it to her. "Read this."

I watch her eyes move over the post, once and then a second time. She sits down on the toilet seat, her hands hanging limply between her knees. "Wow. Nella, you need to talk to him."

My head is moving up and down as I take the phone back, and scroll through the post one more time. I'm in complete disbelief.

When I found out Carter was CJ, it scared and enraged me. It still does. He knows so much, too much, and he might start putting the pieces together.

I would lose him forever if he found out who I am. Except, in his post he talks about me as he once knew me. Maybe things have changed, maybe there is a possibility that Cat might get to meet her father.

"Nella, you need to tell him who you are. I think he deserves to know."

"I know, Grace."

She leaves me in the bathroom, but I follow closely and sit down with Caterina to play. I can figure this out once she's in bed. My head is so full of all these decisions I need to make, and they all have the power to change our lives.

I just don't know whether this change will be for the better.

After I get home from work, I change into clean clothes and give myself a pep talk. Rather than doing my hair and makeup, I throw my hair into a bun on the top of my head and stick my glasses on.

Leaving everything but my keys behind, I walk to his apartment. I try to think about what I'm going to say as I climb the stairs. And as I knock, I realize there is no rehearsal for real life. It doesn't matter how many times I ponder the words; those aren't the ones that will come out.

When the door opens revealing an exhausted looking Carter, all the things I've been practicing in my mind vanish. His eyes widen, but he holds open the door for me with no hesitation.

The apartment he shares with Jaden isn't what I expect. It's fairly tidy and cozy. Their living room is taken up by a huge leather sectional. Edging around it, I sit on the edge with my back facing the large window overlooking the green field I've just crossed.

Carter stands in the middle of the room, looking more nervous than I've ever seen him.

"Do you want something to drink?" His voice is low, a little rumbly, and full of stress.

Shaking my head, I lick my lips and watch him closely as I take a leap of faith. One that could ruin me financially and emotionally.

I don't remove my eyes from his as I leap. "The reason you think you know me from somewhere is because we went to high school together."

He's shaking his head in disbelief. "I know I have my head up my ass a lot of the time, but I swear I would remember you from high school, it wasn't that long ago and there weren't that

many students."

Shoving up from the couch, I move to stand in front of him. My heart races in my chest as I look up at him and reword what I just said. "My given name is Breanne Nella Cooper. After high school, I dropped the Breanne and changed my last name to Anderson, it's my grandmother's last name. I needed a fresh start. I lost some weight, I dyed my hair, I got my braces taken off, and I got contacts. But I am Breanne."

He searches my face. There is no way he can think my words aren't true, how would I know about her otherwise? His hand is shaking as he reaches up and trails his fingers over my cheek.

His face fills with shame as he backs up until the back of his knees hit the couch. He collapses down, his face in his hands.

"Am I so superficial that I didn't even recognize you?" The words are full of loathing.

Moving forward, I sit next to him leaving a safe buffer. "In your defense, you did recognize me, you just didn't know from where."

He looks up at me, his blue eyes so like his daughter's except instead of the happiness that I always see when I look at her, his are dark and sad. "I still should have known. Bre—Nella, I have so much to apologize to you for."

My heart fills with hope. Now that he knows who I am he isn't kicking me out or threatening me with the contract. Folding my hands on my lap, I wait, not quite sure if I should completely let my guard down.

"Let's start with the most recent shitty thing I've done and work backwards." His lips quirk in a smile when I chuckle.

"You know what, I'm going to give you a pass on that one. I think your post is more than enough." In this moment, I don't give a rat's ass about him not telling me. Who is to say I wouldn't do the same thing? All I care about is what this means for me and Cat.

He looks at me skeptically given my response to finding out he is CJ, but accepts the pass. Carter inches closer and takes my hand. "I'm sorry I left that morning without saying goodbye first."

"That really hurt, Carter. You were always so kind to me and then you did that, I don't get why." Removing my hand from his, I stand up and start pacing. "Maybe I was delusional, but I kind of thought I meant more to you than that."

Crossing my arms behind my back, I swallow back the words that I want to say, but can't.

"Nella, I was a kid. My dad called and was reaming me out for not coming home. Then the accusations started because he figured I was with a girl. The things he spewed from his mouth are not words I will repeat to you. I looked down and you were asleep, you looked so peaceful, and I realized I couldn't draw you into my fucked-up family." He comes over to me, giving me my space, but looking into my eyes pleadingly.

Licking my lips, I try to figure out how to get the answers I need without breaching my contract, any more than I probably already have. "We couldn't have stayed friends?"

"That weekend I packed up and left my dad's house. I went on a road trip with some friends and then moved here. When I didn't hear from you, I tried to look you up on Facebook to apologize, but I couldn't find you. Now I know why."

"Didn't hear from me?" My voice is incredulous. He looks at me in confusion when I back away from him, hunching in to protect myself. "I went to your house. I talked to your dad. He told me he passed my message along and that—that you didn't want anything to do with me." *Or Caterina* I mentally scream at him.

My throat feels like it's closing in. I am risking everything being here, admitting who I am, and he's going to play dumb? Maybe I should be grateful. If he continues to play this game maybe he won't come after me for the money I've been paid in child support. At least there's that.

Tears start to form, blurring the room around me. Tilting my head back, I blink at the ceiling until my vision clears.

As I meet his eyes again, I feel the anger I've been letting go resurface. It's better than the breaking of my heart. That small piece that clung to hope that things would change.

How could I be so fucking naive? All this time there was a part of me that held onto the hope that he would change his mind. Or that he would recognize me and realize his mistake. As much as it hurt, I never quit loving him.

"Wait. You came to my house and talked to my dad?"

I give him my best what the hell look. "Uh, yes."

"And he told you I didn't want anything to do with you?"

Nodding, I narrow my eyes on him and he moves into my space and cups my cheeks. I try to turn my head away, but I can't.

"Nella, he never told me you came to see me."

The room spins as I search his eyes for any hint of a lie. All I see is truth.

"What?"

"He didn't tell me you came to see me." Every word is enunciated.

I feel my legs start to shake so I go back to the couch and sit down, tracing my fingertips over the cool leather. The room spins around me. His dad never—he doesn't—he has no clue he has a daughter.

A few choice curse words start running through my mind as I realize the trap I'm now in. I'm still bound by that stupid agreement. One that Carter has no idea about. Well, shit.

"Nella? Are you okay?"

"He lied to me."

Carter doesn't look like this is a surprising revelation. He crouches in front of me, his hands resting on either side of my hips.

"He's not a good person. He's a self-serving, sexist asshole." Carter's voice is a growl, his disregard for his father crystal clear.

This doesn't even feel like real life. Exhaustion hits me in waves, I need time to figure this out. "I always thought—I think I need to go."

Carter doesn't move, his eyes unhappy, his face tense. "Nella, I don't want to let you go. I don't want to deny myself this opportunity to get all of our cards on the table. I want to take you out, get to know you again. You've changed so much in the past two years; you have a kid and I want to learn more about her. I want to learn more about you."

His words are exactly what I want to hear, but it would be living a lie. I can't lay my cards out, not yet.

"Carter—"

He leans forward, his lips touching mine to cut off my words. My body quakes, the sparks flying from his gentle touch igniting a part of me I haven't let loose since that night. With a groan, I wrap my arms around his neck and press into him. His lips move over mine softly, a feeling I have craved since that one night.

Just for one moment I let myself forget what this could cost me. Ever since I met him in the tenth grade, he's been the only man I've seen, the only one I've met in my dreams, and the one whose hold on me has never gone away.

Pulling away, I rest my forehead on his shoulder to catch my breath and clear my head. He intoxicates me, and it would be so easy to give in without regard for the risks.

"Nella, I don't want to ignore this. I'm not going to allow myself to let this feeling pass me by, not without a fight." Carter takes my hands and as he stands pulls me into his arms. He burrows his face into my neck, his hot breath tickling me. "Don't give me an answer. I will pick you up tomorrow evening. I will show you what this could be. Then you can decide what you want."

Breathing in, the smell of fresh laundry and Carter knocks away any common sense that was trying to guide me. "Okay."

CHAPTER 15

CARTER

KENSI OPENS THE door as I'm about to knock. I can't help but look her up and down. She's wearing clothes meant to draw and hold the eye.

"I look hot, right?" She smirks.

"Kens, you know you look good. Date tonight?" I grin back at her; glad she's no longer pissed off at me. I would never admit it, but Kensi kind of scares me and not in the good way that Nella does.

"Not really. I was able to convince Peyton to come out dancing, maybe I will meet someone 'appropriate' as Andie always says." She rolls her eyes as she says appropriate. "In other words, someone boring."

"Appropriate doesn't always mean boring." I point out.

She pats me on the shoulder, shaking her head. "Maybe to some people."

Brushing past me, she sashays down the hall leaving the door to her and Nella's apartment open. I go inside and close it behind me. Soft music plays through the bathroom door, so I sit down on the sofa and scroll through my Tumblr messages.

I feel a little awkward when I receive a message from

someone I know confiding in cjtalks, but today I have a ton of messages about my confession post. Mostly supportive, but the odd one is clearly some troll just looking to make other people miserable.

Shutting down the app when the bathroom door opens, I watch as Nella walks across the hall in a stunning black dress that hugs her curves. She doesn't see me until she comes back from her room sliding earrings into place.

"You're early." She smiles, her features soft in the moment before her guard goes back up. Trying to pursue Nella is going to be a challenge, she's way more complex than any of the other women I've been with.

"I was wearing a path into the carpet so Jaden kicked me out." Shrugging my shoulders, I give her a small smile.

Dimples pop when she gives me a full-on grin, chewing her lower lip as she takes a sweater out of the closet along with her purse. When she turns back to me, the smile is gone. I know she's worried about something, and all I can think about is erasing her concerns and making her see I'm serious about her.

As we walk down the stairs to where my car waits, I resist the urge to hold her hand or press mine into the small of her back. I want to take it slow with her.

We drive to a small cafe in Jasper. It's quiet, with intimate booths, each with art for sale from local artists. The menu is eclectic, and it's not so romantic that it will scare Nella away.

As we settle into the booth, I watch the way the warm lighting catches the subtle red in her hair and makes her chocolate brown eyes even richer.

"What happened to your freckles?" I look at her over my menu, scanning the bridge of her nose for the freckles that were once there.

She looks up from where her eyes were scanning the menu, a faint flush filling her cheeks. "They're still there. I just cover them with foundation."

She goes back to skimming the menu until she finally settles on something and sets it down. I'm still watching her.

"Why do you cover them up?"

"I didn't like the girl I was in high school and at one point I naively thought changing my appearance would be enough. It's not, I know that now, but I guess I've been working on figuring out what I need and not feeling guilty for taking it." She outlines the lettering on her menu, before smiling at me. "I'm a work in progress."

As I listen, I try to connect Nella to the girl I once knew. It's weird to think of them as the same person. Breanne—Nella— somehow I need to leave behind the girl I've missed for two years, and get to know the woman in front of me.

"I'm still the same girl, you know. Names, appearances— child—yes, I've changed, but at the core I am the same person. I struggle with the same insecurities, I still enjoy most of the same things, and there is a part of me that is still just as smitten with you as I was two years ago. Yet I understand if this takes time for you to adjust to. You can ask me whatever you need to, I might not answer everything, but you can ask." She rests her hands on the table, fingers intertwined, as she leans forward and waits.

Licking my lips, I mimic her pose and smirk. "Smitten with me?"

"Shut up." She laughs, her eyes darting away.

"When I look at you, I still see Nella. I guess I'm trying to figure out how you got here." My words are stilted as I try to figure out what I want to say next.

"Maybe instead of trying to determine how we got here, we just start fresh and see what happens."

Nodding, I lean back as the server interrupts us. Nella orders while I scan the menu and select the first thing I see.

After the woman walks away, I lean forward again. "I think that is a smart idea."

"So why don't you want people to know about your blog?"

Grimacing, I clench my hands over the edge of the table, gagging a bit when my thumb brushes against something sticky. Pouring a bit of water onto my napkin, I wipe my hand as I scrunch my face at her. "Just diving right in I see. No, what's your favorite color? Or, what number is on the back of your jersey?"

"Your favorite color is red and your jersey number is eight." She arches a brow at me. "I haven't forgotten those things, Carter. So, let's cut through the bullshit kinds of questions and get to the dirt."

"When did you become so strong and direct?"

"You don't work with one ton animals and not gain confidence. Now stop evading the question." She laughs, the sound a mixture of amusement and irritation.

"I like having a part of myself I don't need to share with people. While I think most of the students around here have a decent head on their shoulders, there is still a big football following and I feel like I'm on display. Especially during the season. The blog is a part of me no one gets to see." She wants everything on the table, so I'm not going to hold back.

Something clicked when I found out she was Breanne; this is my second chance and I'm not going to blow it.

"I get it."

"What about Caterina? Why don't you bring her around?"

Nella straightens in her seat, her spine rigid as her face freezes. She looks almost—scared. "That's not an option for me, I told you that."

"Screw her dad, it's not like we're going to say anything."

She chuckles without humor. "It's a tad more complicated than that. Maybe one day, but for now I need to keep her separate from my life at school."

"Even from Ava, Andie, Kensi, and Peyton?" I push.

"Carter, when it comes to my daughter I will not give in. There are things I need to figure out, consequences that impact not only me and that means any and all decisions I make are not made lightly." She breathes out a sigh of relief when our food appears, digging into the salad she ordered.

Glancing down at my wrap, I sigh and pick it up. It's delicious, but I can't fully enjoy it as I watch Nella stab her fork into her food.

"Don't take out your frustration at me on that poor salad," I say between bites.

She drops her fork into the bowl, cradling her head as she shakes it. "I'm sorry, Carter. I get protective of her and that whole situation is so much more complicated than I can even explain. Let's talk about something else."

Nella is more subdued after the conversation about her daughter, if you can call it that. We move from talking about real stuff to talking about our friends and our plans for the rest of the summer. The confident woman I saw a glimpse of disappears into the quiet, reserved Nella from ten months ago.

I don't like it, and I hate knowing I've just taken massive steps back from any progress we were making.

By the time we're back on campus, I have a sinking feeling that she's not going to want to try giving us a try. When we reach her door, she turns to face me, her eyes a little sad.

"I'm sorry, Carter, Caterina is a sensitive subject for me. I'm not used to talking about her openly, just bear with me while I adjust. I had a nice time." She lifts up onto her toes, pressing a kiss to my cheek. "I'm not sure if it's a good idea for us to pursue a romantic relationship, but I would like to spend more time with you, as friends—if that's okay?"

Her expression is hopeful.

"Of course." Pulling her into my arms, I hug her tightly. "I will take what I can get."

She unlocks her door, giving me a small smile before she shuts it behind her.

My mind works a mile a minute as I make my way home.

There is so much mystery surrounding Nella and her daughter. I feel like there is something obvious that I'm missing, but much like looking at her and not knowing who she was, I can't pinpoint exactly what feels off.

CHAPTER 16

Nella

GRACE WATCHES ME as I pace the apartment. We're supposed to be getting ready to go to Lia's for a picnic, but my anxiety has reared its ugly head and I'm currently falling apart.

"I scoured the contract last night, I don't understand most of it. I need a lawyer. How can I sit across from him again knowing I'm keeping something so huge from him? He wants to date me, and I had to tell him no." Collapsing onto the couch, I stare at the ceiling and count my breaths. "Grace, the only money I save is the money I put away from child support into Cat's savings account. I can't take money from her."

"Nella, put your head between your legs, breathe, and listen." Grace presses her hands into my shoulders, moving my upper body until I'm bent in half. "You have a week until you start working with Lia for the month of August, you can use that to at least hire someone to look over the document. Then you can go from there, you've waited this long what's another month? You need to calm down, Cat is going to wake up from her nap any moment."

When the ringing in my ears passes, I sit up and meet her eyes. "I know. I wish I felt more equipped to deal with this. I wish I knew the right questions to ask, what my rights are, and if there is anything that he can do to me. I'm not completely inept, but when it comes to my rights in this situation, I'm not equipped to deal with this."

Grace grasps my wrists, pulling on them until I stand. She wraps her arms around me, holding me close. "I know, Nell. It's not something anyone your age should be dealing with, hell I'm twenty-six and I don't even have any valuable input. Well, aside from remembering to breathe, and just taking it one day at a time."

She gently pushes me towards Caterina's room, following behind me as I pause at the door before opening it to peer inside. Caterina is playing happily in her crib, but she gives me the biggest smile when she sees me. The feeling is the same every time I look at her, a feeling a gratitude that she's happy and healthy. A feeling of thankfulness that I have a sister who is doing everything she can to help me be able to provide the life I want for Cat.

It doesn't matter what happens as long as she is safe and happy.

Within an hour we're turning onto the driveway leading to Lia's house. It's long and winding, trees lining both sides providing some shade. Grace's eyes widen as she takes in Lia's house and Emma's house.

"If the house she's offering you is even half as gorgeous as these, it's nicer than any place we've ever lived." She gapes out the window as I park next to Lia's SUV.

"They take a lot of pride in their property and treating their staff and animals well, I wouldn't doubt that it's just as beautiful." I help Caterina out of her car seat, setting her on the ground just as Lia comes bounding down the steps.

"I'm so glad you're here!" Lia is all smiles as she hugs me before turning to Grace, "It's so nice to meet you, Grace. Please, make yourself at home."

"Your home is so beautiful." Grace shakes Lia's hand, her eyes widening as she sees the large barn and riding arena by the house.

"We can take the quads out later and take a tour." Lia looks down as Caterina peeks out from behind my legs, a shy smile on her face. "Actually, maybe no quads. Nella, she is the most beautiful little girl I've ever seen."

Dropping my hand to Cat's head, I play with her hair as I beam. "I know."

Lia ushers us into the kitchen where Emma, Dane, Alex, Ryan, and Jesse wait. The table is full of food. Grace looks over her shoulder at me and mouths "oh my god." Grinning, I look at the four very sexy men sitting at the table.

Ryan stands to hold out our chairs, giving me a one-armed hug before he sits next to me. The first time I met Ryan, he came in ranting about the crew building his house. Since then I've realized what a big teddy bear he is and he treats me like he does Lia.

Grace is quiet as we eat, watching all of us interact and laugh. Everyone is entertained by Cat as she attempts to eat but gets most of the food on her face, hands, and clothes. When she's done eating, I attempt to clean her up before giving her a few toys to play with. She settles onto the floor, happily playing while we finish eating.

"She's such a delight, Nella." Alex smirks as he watches her play. His arm wraps around Lia, her hand automatically finding his as she rests her other hand on her belly.

"That's all Grace. She's the one who does the hard work during the week when I'm at school." I set my napkin next to my plate.

"Stop." Grace blushes as everyone looks at her. "She's full of shit. Caterina has the same personality Nella did when she was a baby. It's all her."

We finish eating, Lia shutting down our attempts to help clean up. "Let's show Grace the clinic, and then I want to take you somewhere."

We walk alongside Lia to the clinic, Cat in my arms, as we talk about the different areas of the ranch. When we pass by some foals next to their moms, Cat starts to squeal in excitement.

"I think we have a future cowgirl." Lia smiles as we pause to let Cat check out the babies.

She looks completely entranced, her eyes never leaving one particular foal. "I think so."

When we start to walk again, Cat watches the horses over my shoulder until they disappear behind some trees. It's a short distance to the clinic, Grace's audible gasp when she sees it makes me smile. I had the same reaction when I first saw it.

Lia gives her the same tour I had on my first day. It's weird, seeing it through the eyes of experience. It hasn't lost any of its enormity, though. Instead of going into Lia's office, we head outside so Grace can meet some of the horses we've been working with.

Instead of following, I wander over to the new gelding Lia has assigned to me. He's the first horse I will be working on without her assistance. She will be there to guide me, but I will be doing all the work myself.

"Hey, Sir. You're looking much more settled today." He snorts at me as he goes back to eating his hay.

"This is Sir. He's Nella's first official client. He's kind of an old grump, but I know Nell will win him over," Lia states.

Her confidence in me is one of the reasons I feel like I can accomplish anything. Aside from Grace, no one has ever been so unwavering in their support. She doesn't limit her expectations, and she expects the best, but through her guidance and standards I feel like I've shown myself how capable I am.

Grace links arms with me, Cat now walking in front of us as we follow Lia into her office. My eyes are on Cat as I walk into the spacious room, but I feel Grace and Lia looking at me so I glance up to see why they're staring.

The office is completely rearranged to make room for a second desk, a desk that has a frame with two photos on it, one of me working with a horse and the second of me riding Ollie.

The rest of the desk is bare, waiting for me to add my personal touch.

"Alex and I thought that you should have your own space. You will be here five days a week soon." Lia's eyes are full of unshed tears. She giggles and kind of waves her hands in the air. "Sorry, I think my pregnancy hormones are kicking in."

I walk over and give her a hug, the words I need to say escaping me until Grace coughs a little. "Thank you so much. You have no idea how much you, and this job, mean to me."

We both laugh, swiping our fingers under our eyes before Lia walks to the door. "I have one more thing I want to show you."

Grace and I exchange looks as we follow Lia out the door. She leads us down a path, one I've never been down. As we pass the building site of Ryan's house, I point it out to Grace. "That's Ryan's house. He was banned from the building site for a while when he tried to take over the contractor's job."

Lia turns and starts walking backwards, smirking. "That's my big brother. He's protective of this property and everyone on it. He can be so gruff and abrupt, but underneath he's soft and squishy."

We walk for around ten minutes until we enter a clearing where the cutest little house sits facing a road that looks like it leads to the driveway for the clinic. It's a bungalow style farmhouse with a wraparound porch. Everything about it is immaculate from the blue siding, to the freshly stained wood of the porch.

It's like I woke up and realized my dream home is real. The yard is full of flowers and mature trees, all maintained to perfection.

"I know you want to see how August goes, but I talked about it with Dane and Ryan, if you want to move in here for the month you are more than welcome." Lia hands me a key. "Go look, I will meet you back at the clinic."

Caterina lifts her arms up asking me to pick her up. Gently lifting her, I settle her onto my hip before heading up the porch steps to the front door. Grace follows me inside, shutting the front door behind us.

The interior of the house is stunning. An open concept home with vaulted ceilings. The living room and kitchen are open to each other, the walls a soft gray but offset with teal and purple throw pillows on the dark gray couch. Dark chestnut cabinets offset gorgeous granite counter tops in varying shades of silver and white.

Laying Caterina on the couch, she curls up and falls asleep as Grace and I make our way wordlessly through the home. There are three bedrooms and two bathrooms. All furnished and stunning.

The house is perfect. I leave Grace to explore the kitchen, making my way into the basement only to discover a massive laundry room in one corner while the rest of the basement is open and set up as a play area. This had to have been done with Cat in mind, a blanket fort taking up half the space while the other half has cubbies for toys, a table for crafts, and a huge box of stuffed animals.

Grace finds me sitting on the floor, a bear wrapped in my arms.

"This house is—"

"Incredible."

Light shines in through the full windows warming the room. "I want to live here, Grace. I want Caterina to grow up in this home, with all this space around her. I want to see her every day and to go to a job I know I love. I'm still going to see how August goes, but I think we should take Lia's offer on staying here for the month."

Grace looks around before turning shining eyes on me. "If we move in here, you know you're not going back to school, right?"

With a chuckle, I stand and toss the bear back into his spot before pushing myself off the floor. "I know."

We make our way upstairs, picking Cat up before locking up

on our way out. Grace and I don't need to talk about things any more, I already know that she is on board to do whatever it takes to make me happy. One day I will be able to repay her for everything she has done.

I'm throwing things from my closet into my suitcase when Carter comes into my room with Chinese takeout and a pitcher of iced tea. I stop what I'm doing so I can gape at him when he spreads out a blanket on the floor.

"What are you doing?"

"You need to stop and eat, you've been packing all day and Kensi said that you haven't eaten yet." He takes my hand and leads me to the food, gently pushing down on my shoulders.

He settles next to me opening containers, the delicious scent from the food causes my stomach to growl. When I got home from Lia's last night, I went right into productivity mode. Grace needs my help to pack, so instead of spacing it out over the week until we move in to the farmhouse this weekend, I have today for myself and the rest of the week to help Grace.

Kensi tried to be supportive and excited for me, but I know she's struggling with the idea of living here alone. It's one more thing to feel guilty over. At least I will be present in Cat's life on a daily basis that strikes something off the growing list.

We eat in silence, Carter seems to be aware that I have a lot on my mind and is letting me reside there. It hurts to look at him, knowing what he wants from me that I can't give him while I'm keeping something so important from him. In my spare time, I've been looking online at different lawyers, but they're all way too expensive.

"You look too worried for someone who is packing to move into a gorgeous house—yes, Kensi told us all about it this afternoon. What's going on in there?" He sets his plate aside, holding my gaze with a firm expression.

"I feel bad for leaving Kensi, but relieved because I get to see Cat and Grace every day." Shrugging, I look at him and push forward. "And I'm exploring the legal grounds I have to talk with Cat's father about her. There have been some new developments and I want to see what I can do with the information without risking Cat's well-being."

Pain blooms in my chest, the urge to confess what's going on crushing me. This secret is going to blow up in my face, I know it is, but my fear of Marshall locks the words up tight.

"New developments?"

"Yeah, it's even more complicated."

"Talk to me." He presses.

"It turns out he doesn't know he has a daughter." I look straight at him. It wouldn't be a stretch for him to figure out Cat could be his. I don't think that would prevent the hurt and betrayal, but it's better than holding this in any longer.

His mouth gapes open as he processes that. "I don't get it. Didn't the contract you sign state he didn't want contact?"

"Yep."

"But now you find he doesn't know?"

"Yep."

"That's—complicated."

Dropping my plate onto the blanket, I tuck my hair behind my ears and sigh. "I know."

Chewing on my lip, I try to focus on the fact that by the end of August, I will be able to afford a lawyer and then I can finally figure out how to get everything out in the open. Until then, I just need to keep my feelings for Carter in check. As I gaze up at him, my chest hurts for a whole different reason. The way he's looking at me is the way I've dreamed about for two years.

Averting my gaze, I wipe my hands on a napkin before tidying up our dishes. Carter stands, holding his hand out to me forcing me to meet his gaze once more as I slip my hand into his. He pulls me up, releasing me as I stand. As I turn to go back to my closet, my feet tangle in the blanket we were just seated on. My body propels forward but before I hit the floor, Carter's arms wrap around me, my body crushing into the firm muscles of his chest.

Air rushes from my lungs as he holds me closer to him instead of letting me go, his pupils dilating as I search his eyes. My hands slide up to his chest, fisting his shirt as I lift onto my toes and press my lips to his.

With a moan, he wraps his hand around the back of my neck, pressing my body even closer into his, and devours me. That's the only way to describe the way his lips move across mine. I feel cherished and wanted, every bit of self-preservation I was holding on to dissipates as he deepens the kiss, his tongue stroking over mine. The hardness of his erection presses into my belly, my head a little dizzy as I imagine him stripping me down and taking me on my bedroom floor.

A whimper escapes my lips when he pulls away, dropping his arms when he's sure I won't stumble again. Our chests rise and fall rapidly as we stare at each other. Carter growls in frustration before stepping into me, moving me until my back hits the wall before his lips slam onto mine once again.

We are a clash of teeth and tongues and moans as all of the tension we've been holding back is unleashed. Pressing into Carter, I revel in the feel of his lips on mine. The man can kiss and even if this doesn't go any further, I could go on kissing him forever.

This time when we stop for air he doesn't move away. His blue eyes sparkle as his thumb makes circles on my shoulder. "Are you sure dating is off the table? I don't want to treat you like a one-night stand, and you're definitely more than a friend with benefits. Nella, let's try this. I want to be more."

Dropping my forehead to his chest, I try to find the strength to do what's right, but as I look up and see a sexy little smirk as he waits for me to give him an answer I ignore the smart choice and say, "Okay."

Carter is kissing me again before I can say anything else, his hands firmly on my hips as he takes his time to explore my lips.

Kissing him is incredible and I don't want to stop, but part of me finds little joy in this moment because it feels incomplete and dishonest.

CARTER
August

MY NAPKIN FALLS from my fingers to my plate as I set it on the coffee table. We're having a movie night but it's not the same without Nella. She's been at her new place for a weekend and we already feel her absence. Usually she would be home by now, sitting amongst our group smiling and talking.

Since we've sorted through all the secrets she's much more open and relaxed. Now she's gone. Kensi is oddly quiet, the dark shadows under her eyes show the impact of Nella's loss.

In fact, our entire social group is unusually subdued.

Me: Everyone is missing you tonight. I miss you.

Tipping my beer, I down the rest before slamming the bottle onto the coffee table. Ignoring Andie's glare, I look around the room. "Okay, we all miss Nella, but we need to stop sulking. How do you think she would feel knowing we're sitting here moping?"

"The apartment is so empty," Kensi sighs. "But you're right. I'm happy for her and this amazing opportunity."

My phone dings with an incoming text, suddenly it feels like

I'm a baby deer surrounded by a pack of wolves.

"Is that Nella?"

"How is she?"

"When can we go to her house?"

Glancing down, I feel a mixture of excitement and disappointment when I see it's my brother. "It's Billy."

The energy in the room deflates once again, but we start the movie and soon lose ourselves in the story.

Over an hour passes before Nella finally texts me back.

> **Nella:** I miss you all too. We just finished unpacking and getting everything settled. Cat loves her play room in the basement. She fell asleep down there tonight. What are you all doing?
>
> **Me:** Watching a movie. Kensi keeps checking her phone to see if you've texted her.
>
> **Nella:** Crap, I meant to message her earlier.
>
> **Me:** I'm sure she understands; you're just getting settled and you're now working full-time.
>
> **Nella:** I know, it's definitely a different feeling.
>
> **Me:** It feels weird here without you too.

We talk back and forth, smiles erupting on everyone's faces as Nella finally texts them as well, which means no one is paying much attention to the movie. I can tell the exact moment Nella informs the rest of the women that we kissed and are going to try being a couple. Four heads pop up and turn to stare at me.

With a dramatic sigh, I drop my head back and stare at the ceiling. "Let me have it."

When nothing is said after a few moments, I lift my head and look at four very different reactions to the news ranging from amusement to concern.

"We don't need to say anything, because you already know what's at stake. It would be redundant to threaten you with anything when the worst punishment of you screwing this up is you lose Nella," Andie speaks up.

The others nod. Licking my lips, I check to see if Nella has replied to my latest text. I've already lost her from my life once, I won't lose her again.

"You've been living in your place for a week now, when do we get to come over for a housewarming party?" I hand Nella her coffee, taking a sip of my mocha.

"Oh, well, I wasn't really planning on having a housewarming party. It doesn't make sense for all of you to drive out to the ranch when I can drive to campus." Nella avoids my gaze as she walks through the door I'm holding for her.

Her hand is cold when I take it. She finally looks up at me when I lead her in the opposite direction of where we need to go.

"Aren't we going to Andie and Lucas' place?"

"Not yet. I want some time with you before I need to share you." Smiling when her cheeks flush, I give her hand a gentle squeeze. "Why don't you want us to come visit you?"

"Carter, it's just—Cat. I'm not ready." She glances away from me as she talks.

"You're lying. You don't live on campus anymore, why do you feel you need to hide her from us?" Her face flushes more as I press on. "It's not like you're the only one in our group who has a kid. Noah is regularly around us and he's still a well-adjusted, happy kid. So, what's the deal? Why don't you want us to meet your daughter?"

She pulls her hand out of mine, hugging her arms across her chest. "Please, just drop it."

"As your friend, and more importantly someone who wants to be a big part of your life, I want to know why you won't let me or your best friends in."

"I said drop it." Her voice lowers as she practically snarls at me.

"And I'm not going to. Being closed off isn't the best way to start this relationship. And you wanted to 'dig in' when we went out, so let's dig in. Why can't I meet her?" I move to stand in front of her, cupping her cheek so she has to look up at me.

Nella's eyes glisten, her lips trembling. "Because she's *your* fucking daughter!"

She backs away from me, slapping her hand over her mouth as the tears she was holding back fall free. Her lips move as she whispers "oh no" over and over again. My hand is suspended in the air where seconds ago it had been on her cheek as I stare at her.

Cat is mine?

How? I was only with Nella once.

All of our conversations about Caterina flash through my mind. The absent father. The contract about never contacting the father. How he didn't want to know his own kid, but then he never knew about her.

I count how many months after Nella and I had sex that Caterina was born, my stomach roiling as I finally put everything together. My knees give out and I crumple to the ground, I cradle my head in my hands as I try to clear my head and think through this logically. But how do you think through news like this logically? Here I am thinking all our secrets are out in the open and she's holding onto a huge one.

I can feel myself getting to the point of exploding. The sense of betrayal strong. There is no way I can look or speak to Nella when I feel like this so I run my hands through my hair and close my eyes. We need to deal with this now, I'm not about to walk away and let her go into hiding. It's not like I know where she's living. So, I need to calm the fuck down.

Gripping my arms, I squeeze until my hands hurt.

With a deep breath, I look up at Nella in a mixture of confusion and anger. "Why the fuck didn't you tell me? We've been hanging out for almost a year."

She drops down next to me, inhaling a shaky breath. "You have every right to be pissed off, but I've already told you why. Just remember when I was Breanne and you were CJ that you understood."

"Yeah, I get it, you thought I wanted nothing to do with her, but what about when you found out I had no clue? You could have told me then." When her tears continue to fall, I feel the anger dissipate, how can I hang on to it when it's obvious she's hurting as badly as me. Of course, it hurts that she didn't tell me, but I know her reasons why. I just wish she knew she could trust me enough to know I wouldn't betray her.

"I wanted to. It's something I've been struggling with ever since I found out you had no clue. But under the weight of the guilt was an overwhelming fear at what I would be risking and that's Cat's security. Marshall pays me two thousand dollars a month. Three quarters of that goes to Grace and it barely covers her bills. The other five hundred I put into a bank account for Cat. I can't afford to pay him back." Her hands shake as she gestures, trying to explain and appease me.

"I guess I understand why you didn't tell me, but it doesn't mean I'm not hurt by it. I feel betrayed by my father, and I've missed the first year and a half of my own daughter's life. I know I haven't always been the best guy, but I never thought I would be *that* guy." Reaching my hand out, I brush the tears from her cheeks.

"I never wanted to keep her from you."

"I want to be a part of her life."

"I know and you can be. As soon as you want."

Standing, I brush the seat of my jeans off before helping her off the ground. "We should go to Lucas and Andie's. They will be wondering where we are."

When I go to walk, she holds me back. "I think you should meet Cat before we tell them any of this."

Nodding, I take her hand and we walk to see our friends. My entire world has changed in the blink of an eye.

I have a kid. I went from just starting to date the one that got away, to having a child with her. My chest tightens as I think about the person responsible for this. My damn father, the man who only thinks about himself. I've never hated the man more than I do right now.

"I want you to know that you don't need to worry about money anymore."

"Carter, I don't care about that. I just want you to know Cat."

Stopping her outside her former apartment building, I grip her shoulders and look into her eyes. "I am her father, in every sense of the word. This means looking after her and you."

By the time we make it to the outside of our friends' apartment, I turn Nella towards me. I could feel Nella watching me the entire way up the stairs, the strain obvious from the tenseness in her arm and posture. She's a little flushed as she gazes up at me, but otherwise the redness around her eyes is gone. Tucking her hair behind her ears, I lean down and brush my lips over hers.

"We're going to get through this."

"I know."

"I don't think you do, but I will show you. Are you ready for our meddling friends?"

She chuckles and shakes her head. "Today will be nothing compared to when they find out my daughter is also your daughter."

"Maybe we should go on Maury."

"We're not dramatic enough."

"I'm sure we could change that."

The door swings open to reveal Andie. We're laughing as she stands there and gapes at us. Nella walks in and give her a hug. I follow behind with a wink.

We ignore the eyes of our friends as I take her hand and we settle next to each other on the couch. Nella smirks a little as I wrap my arm over her shoulder and looks get exchanged.

Finally, I chuckle and shake my head. "Out with it. Thought bubbles are about to sprout from your heads."

"It's just weird, you two have been skirting this for a long time and now you're incredibly comfortable around each other." Ava sits on Dax's knee as she watches us.

Nella looks at me before turning back to our friends. "Sometimes things just click. It helps that we went to high school together."

"What?" Kensi's voice is shrill.

Nella looks at me, so I fill them in on the rest of the story. We don't tell them about Cat or the drama with my father, but we fill them in on the rest of our story. By the time we're done, I don't think I've ever talked so much about myself.

These people are my family and I want them to know me, all of me, and I think Nella feels the same way. People have an interesting tendency not to open up about things, even to those closest to them, in an attempt to protect themselves. I know I don't feel like I need to protect myself from my friends.

Once I meet Cat, we can lay all of our cards on the table and life will finally be looking up again.

CHAPTER 18

Nella

MY FOOT BOBS in the air as I channel surf, I need something to distract me from watching the clock. Grace walks past snatching the remote out of my hand and changing the channel to the Disney Channel.

Shoving up from the couch, I walk to the front window and pull the curtain back so I can look down the winding driveway. With a sigh, Grace is at my back with her hands on my shoulders as she guides me away from the window and over to the bench by the front door.

"I know you're nervous, but he's not supposed to be here for another hour. Why don't you go to the clinic and help Lia with the paperwork you know she's been putting off?" Her eyes sparkle with humor as she hands me my boots and supervises me putting them on with her arms crossed.

"I don't think this is a good idea. I'm not focused enough."

Grace shakes her head and opens the door. "Tough. You need something to distract you and you're getting Caterina worked up."

She's right, Cat has been fussing all day and it's because I've been cleaning and pacing and then cleaning the same things over and over. Carter is coming to meet her and I'm terrified. What if he meets her and decides it's too much? What if Marshall finds out? That man terrifies me.

The words *what if* run through my head in dozens of different scenarios in the brief time it takes to walk to the clinic. Lia glances up from her desk, smirking when she sees me.

"Grace kicked me out."

Lia doesn't say anything, she just tosses a folder onto my desk and gets back to work. With one last look out the door, I shut it behind me and take a seat.

We work in silence for a while, Lia getting up and disappearing for a bit as I type out a report from the notes Lia took this week. A steaming mug of tea appears on my desk before Lia drops back into her seat.

Finishing up the first report, I print it off to add to the file before emailing a copy to the client. Leaning back in my chair, I pick up my mug and take a small sip.

"Nella, you need to take the pressure of today off you, Carter, and Cat." She drops her free hand to her stomach as she watches me.

"I know. He just took it so well, I guess I'm waiting for the other shoe to drop." Looking down into my mug, I blow gently to cool off the hot drink to a more bearable temperature. When Lia doesn't say anything, I glance back up at her.

Her lips are pursed, creases lining her forehead as she thinks. "Okay, I was going to say something, but it slipped my mind."

"Baby brain."

"What?"

"It's baby brain. You're going to forget things more and more, it's frustrating as hell."

We laugh, and for the first time all day I relax a little.

"I wish my story was a little more like yours. I don't regret Cat, but we're still so young and I feel so unequipped to deal with all the possible ways this can go wrong."

"Look, things can go wrong no matter what stage in life you're at. And considering how young you are, you're incredibly strong. Just take it one step at a time. And don't worry too much about the things you can't control. Life is too short to dwell on that stuff."

Standing from my seat, I walk around the desk and give her a hug. "Thank you."

We dive back into the reports and before I know it, the time has come for me to head home and introduce Carter to his daughter. Lia gives me an encouraging smile as I head out the door.

By the time I get home, Carter is standing next to his car checking out the house. He turns when he hears my boots crunching on the gravel, a tight smile on his face as he meets me half way.

"I don't think I've ever been so nervous in my entire life."

Wrapping my arms around his waist, I rest my chin on his chest and look up at him. "That makes two of us. And I had to tell your dad I was pregnant."

"Let's not talk about that asshole right now. We need to talk about the contract later, just not now." He hugs me to him, enveloping me into the safe cocoon of his arms.

Together we turn to the house and start walking. Linking my fingers with his, I squeeze tightly as I open the front door. Carter's eyes find Caterina right away. She's sitting in front of the couch on the floor with her blocks, babbling away. Grace is in the kitchen getting her lunch ready, but she turns to give us both a warm smile. Carter doesn't even notice.

"She looks like you," he whispers. Her head is bent as she plays, so all he can see is the crown of her head and the dark auburn hair that matches mine.

Humming, I sit down and take my boots off before going to kneel in front of her. She looks up at me with those brilliant blue eyes and smiles. Carter gasps behind me and she finally notices him. Her lips form an "O" as she watches him over my shoulder.

I lift her to her feet, her eyes never moving from him.

"You can come in here." I look over my shoulder and grin at him. He looks awestruck as he shoves his shoes off and creeps over, his eyes never leave Cat. "She has my hair, but everything else is you."

He drops to the floor next to me, his side pressing into mine. Cat is still staring at Carter, her eyes wide as she watches him watch her, one hand practically shoved in her mouth.

"Hi Cat." Carter's voice is rough with emotion. He clears his throat and glances at me before looking back to her.

My eyes well with tears as she removes her fist from her mouth and gives him a toothy grin as she holds her sopping wet fist out for him to bump. His giant fist taps lightly against hers. She bends and picks up some blocks handing them to him.

"I'm going to let you play with her while I help Grace with lunch."

Before I can stand, he pulls me to him and kisses me on the lips with a soft brush of his. Caterina babbles away as they start to play, Carter's deep voice talking back as he holds the blocks she hands him.

I watch them as I cut up veggies. Every few minutes, Carter looks up at me, the joy in his eyes makes my heart pound with emotion.

Grace leans against the counter next to me. "That boy looks at you like he loves you."

"Don't be silly. It's too soon."

"Maybe he's loved you for as long as you've loved him." She pushes away from the counter as the timer beeps. The scent of homemade pizza filling the room as she takes it out of the oven.

Her words are meant to fill me with optimism, but I refuse to let myself be disappointed by getting my hopes up for something that can take years. I've loved Carter since high school, but I don't expect him to reciprocate those feelings any time soon. Our path to this point hasn't been smooth and I don't anticipate it to get any easier. Lia was right that we shouldn't dwell on what we can't control, but that doesn't mean I'm going to be unrealistic.

"Cat, come get your lunch." Cat gets up, wobbling a little as she walks over to her chair. Carter follows behind her and lifts her into the chair. I smile as he tries to figure out the buckles, but don't interrupt. I know he likes to figure things out for himself.

The proud look on his face when he finally gets it reminds me of when I first had Cat and I was figuring everything out. I wish he could have been there for her first milestones.

He must see the sad look on my face because he comes over and pulls me into him and kisses the top of my head, before going to help Grace set the table. We sit on opposite sides of Cat, Grace joining us in conversation as we eat.

She never met Carter since she was already done school by the time I was in the tenth grade. As we eat and talk, I look around me and see a future. If we can work through all the secrets and deal with the looming threat of his father, I feel like nothing is out of our reach. Even if our relationship doesn't work, I can see that Carter will be a great father to Cat. That's all I've ever wanted.

"Do you want to walk around the property and meet Lia? Grace always takes Cat for a walk after lunch." I get up from the table and start cleaning up. Before I have the chance to, Carter is wiping Caterina's hands and face.

"I would like that." The smile he gives me takes my breath away. It's a little bit cocky, but underneath that is pure happiness. I don't remember ever seeing him smile quite like this.

We finish cleaning up and then head out to explore the property. Leading Carter around the house, I point out the things I would add to the yard if we were to stay.

"Lia told me we can use as much space as we want and they will put in anything we desire." Taking his hand, I turn us towards the clinic.

"It sounds like they really want you to stay." His tone of voice is strange and his face doesn't give me a clue about what's going on in his head, but I know I need to tread carefully.

"I guess so. I think they're just good to the people they employ." Shrugging, I point towards Ryan's house as we pass. "That's where Lia's eldest brother will live as soon as his house is done."

Carter checks everything out, asking questions as we walk. I know the moment he sees the massive building through the trees because he freezes in place.

Cat takes advantage of the fact I've let her hand go and starts picking up pine cones. She walks over to Carter and holds one up for him. When he takes it she lifts her arms. "Up."

He smiles softly, bending to lift her into his arms as we start walking again.

"This facility is state of the art. Lia and Ryan have clients that come from all over, including from Montana and Idaho, just for their services. Ryan is one of the top farriers in North America, and Lia's services are so specialized that she has to turn people away."

As we pass the entrance to Ryan's shop, he appears in the doorway. He's wearing his chaps and his button-down shirt is open. Heat wafts through the open door.

When Cat sees him she squeals and leans towards him, her arms open.

"Hey, pretty girl!" He takes Cat from Carter who looks like someone kicked his puppy. "Darlin.'" Ryan reaches out to tug on my pony tail.

"Ryan, this is Carter, Cat's dad. Ryan is Lia's eldest brother."

The two men size each other up as they reach out to shake hands. Ryan grunts out a greeting before returning his attention to Cat. He blows a raspberry on her cheek before setting her down. With one last tug on my pony tail, he turns back into his workshop and shuts the door.

Cat waddles towards the door leading to the office I share with Lia, oblivious to the tension rolling off Carter.

"He seems—nice," Carter growls. Despite his obvious irritation at Ryan, his grasp on my hand is gentle.

Chuckling, I open the door to the office. Cat goes racing inside to her toy corner. Lia looks up from her paperwork and leans back in her chair, a knowing grin spreading when she sees the look on Carter's face.

"I see you met my delightful brother." She stands up and crosses the room. "You weren't lying, Nella, Caterina sure takes after him."

Giggling as the annoyed look leaves Carter's face for one of amusement, I nod.

"You must be Lia. I'm glad to see you're more pleasant than your brother." Carter shakes her hand. He looks around the office, taking in my desk and the photo of me riding Ollie that Lia gave me.

"He's just protective of us girls. It's not personal, he just doesn't know you. If he hadn't known Alex for a year by the time he found out about us, I'm sure Alex would have gotten the same reception." Lia straightens the papers on her desk. "Are you getting the tour?"

"Yes, and then it's time for Caterina's nap."

"Well, get out then." She winks and waves her hands at us.

I lead Carter through the same tour Lia gave me and Grace. He has the exact same look of awe that I had and that Grace had when she saw the set up.

As we walk back to the house, we each take one of Caterina's hands and swing her between us. Her laughter is contagious and by the time we get back to the house my cheeks hurt from smiling so much.

CHAPTER 19

CARTER

IT'S ALMOST TOO much to tear my eyes away from Cat as she sleeps. When I first pulled up to Nella's house, I was so terrified that I almost turned around and went back to campus, but I'm not a coward and I needed to meet her.

I've spent less than five hours with her and I can't believe how much I love her already. Nella says she looks like me, but I see so much of Nella in her too. She's perfect. All the worries and doubts that I would feel connected with this little girl have evaporated. Maybe it's just in my head, but there is a connection there I could never have anticipated.

Nella shuts the door and leads me into the bedroom next to Cat's. She sits on the foot of the bed, crossing her legs, and watching me as I wander around.

The room is cozy, the walls covered in photos of Caterina. It's like a timeline on her wall.

"She's so perfect, Nella. You've done an amazing job with her and I'm so sorry things went the way they did, but you really didn't need me, did you?"

"I couldn't have done it without Grace, she's been my rock and has sacrificed so much for us. And you're wrong, I did need

you I just made it work without you. I still need you and so does Cat." She pats the bed next to her, taking my hand when I sit down. "How are we going to deal with him?"

Her face is strained with the weight of my father's threat looming over her. It's not something I'm worried about, I know enough to know the fact he kept this from me will most likely nullify the contract she signed, but this is something she's been living with for almost three years.

Loathing fills me as I think about what that man has kept from me, what I've missed out on because of him. I left her that morning because of him, and I lost out on knowing my child because of him.

Tossing my bag out the door, I cross my arms as Dad tries to intimidate me.

"I'm going to give you one last chance to rethink an internship at my company rather than traipsing across the country with your idiot friends." His voice is eerily calm; he honestly thinks the threat of cutting me off will change my mind.

I don't want his fucking money; I don't need it. "Yeah, I'm not changing my mind."

"Boy, you listen here. I am your father and you will speak to me with respect."

"Seriously? Respect is earned. I'm done doing your bidding, I've already lost enough because of it." Slinging my bag over my shoulder, I turn away.

He barks out a laugh, following me to my car as he snarls at me. "Trust me, you've lost nothing. I've saved you from making foolish mistakes."

Opening my car door, I toss my bag in the back and glare at him. His idea of saving me is delusional. We've been arguing all morning, ever since I walked in the door after leaving Breanne.

My chest aches at the thought of her, but maybe this time I saved her. Saved her from being let down by me more than waking up alone, because all I ever hear is how much of a disappointment I am. Sliding into my seat, I slam my door and back out of my spot without looking at my father again.

Pausing, I look down to where my fingers are entwined with

Nella's and I sigh. This is all my fault. He may be the influence behind all of the things I've missed out on but it's only because I *let* him. Isn't that the clincher? At the end of the day, we choose who impacts us. We make choices and live with those decisions. It's because of my choices that we are here now, Nella looking on the verge of tears at the fear of having to pay back money she doesn't have.

"Nella, take away the fear he's shoved down your throat and think about the situation. He has no grounds. And if he tries to take you to court, I will counter-sue him. I will confront him regardless, but you have no need to answer to him anymore." Giving her hand a gentle squeeze, I watch her face shift from an expression of concern to one I haven't seen on her face ever. It's a look I'm familiar with, but this time it feels completely different.

Maybe it's because it's the one person who has haunted me looking at me in the way that wakes my cock up that's caused the shift. My body knows what it wants to do, but my mind is telling me not to rush anything.

When she leans in to kiss me, I let her take the lead until she's straddling me and grinding her hips into me, so similar to that night so long ago. Her moans fill my head with fog, but I manage to pull away, hands holding her hips still as I try to hold onto the control I'm clinging to.

"Nella, I'm hanging by a thread here, if you keep this up you're going to be naked on this bed under me screaming my name." My voice is deeper than usual, thick with need for her.

She hums, pressing into me, her lips trailing up my neck. "And that's bad because . . ."

I groan as she continues to trail her lips over my skin, my restraint rapidly dissipating. "Because of respect and . . ." Swallowing hard when she grinds her palm over my erection, I push through the temptation and croak out, "Taking it slow."

Nella groans in frustration as she presses her palms into my shoulders and shoves me down onto her bed. "Listen, I appreciate what you're trying to do, but we've been together before and I know I'm not like the other girls you've hooked up with, something I can tell is weighing on you."

She leans down taking advantage of my surprise to kiss me, her tongue stroking mine as her hands slide up under my shirt and over my abs. My muscles tense and twitch with the soft touch of her fingers. I guide her hips, my cock straining against my jeans begging to be released.

When she pulls away, her fingers unbuttoning my jeans as she smiles down at me, I smirk. "Were you this confident with the other guys you've been with?"

Her eyes drop to where her fingers are now fiddling with my zipper, her cheeks flushing red as she licks her lips and looks back up at me. "What other guys?"

Those three words steal my breath. *Holy shit.* I've never felt possessive of the women I've been with, they were a way to pass the time, but knowing Nella hasn't been with anyone else since me makes my lips spread into a wide grin. At the same time, it makes taking this step with her again as important as it was the first time.

My first instinct is to ask why, but some blood returns to my brain and I realize what a stupid question that is. Licking my lips, I wrap my hand around the back of her neck and pull her down for a kiss.

This kiss is different than the ones leading to this point. Without words, I'm trying to tell her how much remorse I have for leaving her that day and how much I've missed her. Mixed in there is guilt for how I've moved from woman to woman while she has cared for our daughter. And a small part of me kisses her a little harder because I'm worried she will regret not experiencing more and resent me for the number of sexual partners I've had.

I've never been good at expressing my feelings, I force myself with Nella because I know it's important and I don't want communication issues to plague our relationship. This kiss gives me time to figure out how to express all of this delicately.

Nella rests her hands on my hips, letting me lead the kiss until I'm ready to say the words. When she pulls back, I swipe my thumb over her lower lip as I form the words I need to say and she needs to hear. "I don't want you to regret missing out on dating, or resent me for my—history. Especially since I'm the cause to you needing to sacrifice a normal post high school experience."

She starts laughing drawing my eyes to the way her tits move. I'm such an ass, but half my brain is still focusing on where her body is touching mine.

"Post high school experience?" She snorts as she inhales a laugh, her face turning even redder as she laughs harder. "Carter, I think we both know in the grand scheme of things, our dating history is not important. I don't care about any of that, I care about you. Maybe in the moment I would get jealous and angry, but it's because there were so many things unsaid."

"I just . . ."

"Look, I promise to tell you if I start to feel any of those things." She runs her fingers through my hair before leaning back down.

Before our lips have a chance to touch, the sound of Caterina babbling comes through the baby monitor on Nella's bedside table. She scrunches her eyes shut and groans, pressing her forehead to mine.

When those stunning brown eyes open to look into mine, they're filled with frustration and humor. With a groan, she pushes away from me, straightening her clothes. "Shall we?"

Glancing down at the hard ridge in my jeans, I smirk up at her. "I might need a moment."

Nella chuckles before turning to the door and disappearing into the hall. Ignoring the ache in my balls, I stand and follow her into Cat's room. When those sweet blue eyes that match my own find me, my chest aches. If I'm totally honest, the idea of being a parent was something that never crossed my mind, but then I met this sweet little girl and I can feel my whole mentality beginning to shift.

I watch as Nella lifts Cat out of her crib and carries her to a changing table on the opposite side of the room. The entire time that she's laying there her eyes are on me. I wonder if I feel as familiar to her as she does to me, even though that sounds impossible, it's like there is an invisible connection.

Shaking my head, I internally roll my eyes. Wishful thinking. My childhood is a prime example that parenting and connecting with your children isn't an inherent instinct. It takes work just like any other relationship.

"Come take her, I need to use the bathroom." Nella stands with Cat until I've lifted her in my arms. I make my way into the living room where Grace is sitting on the couch reading.

Even when we were in high school I knew next to nothing about Nella's family. I never met Grace or saw her parents. Giving her a nervous smile, I set Caterina on the floor by her toys and join Grace on the couch.

Without Nella here as a buffer, I try to think of something, anything, to say. I don't know what she thinks of me or our situation, I can't imagine it was positive prior to Nella finding out my father kept me in the dark. Licking my lower lip, I glance towards the hall for Nella.

"Carter, there is no reason to be nervous around me. I'm supportive of your involvement with my sister and niece. I've been telling Nella to bite the bullet and open up to you, I never trusted your father and the stipulations he enforced through that horrendous contract."

Those dark brown eyes, full of compassion, hold mine until I finally relax.

"Thank you. Trust me, if I had known, nothing would have stopped me from being involved."

She smiles at me, the warmth from that gesture reminds me of my brother and the fact I need to tell him what's going on. This is life changing and if I'm being honest I'm still wrapping my head around everything.

The couch dips next to me as Nella sits down. Her hand comes to rest on my thigh as she leans into me. Her words from earlier resound in my head as she shows me affection without restriction. It's clear she truly meant what she said, she's not going to let our history impact our relationship now and how it moves forward.

Our whole situation could explode into chaos if we let it, but Nella is making it simple and easy. It doesn't escape me how lucky I am that she is the mother of my child. I can't ever take that for granted.

Small hands press into my knees as Caterina captures my attention from my thoughts and the light conversation between Nella and Grace.

"Up." She lifts her arms so I can pick her up and set her on my knee. One small hand reaches out to play with the zipper on my hoody, her face completely enthralled with the shiny silver teeth opening and closing.

She starts babbling, small words interspersed with gibberish that no one can understand. Cat seems to have a significant vocabulary for a child her age. Nella and Grace watch us as Caterina talks to me for a bit before getting up to start cooking dinner.

Hardly any time seems to pass before dinner is on the table and I'm once again sitting with Caterina between Nella and me as we eat. Conversation flows easily. I haven't had this sense of family since Billy and Natalie moved.

After dinner is finished, I help clean up before following Nella to bathe Caterina. Once again, she lets me take charge while she sits back and watches. It can't be easy when she has spent the majority of the past year away from Cat to step aside and let me do this, but she does.

It's as I'm bathing Cat and talking with Nella about their various routines they've established here that I realize she won't be coming back to school. She will stay here with Caterina where

she can finally be with Caterina every day.

I also realize that means if I want to be a part of their lives, I need to evaluate how my career will fit in, considering how remote of an area it is. Until now, I always figured I would move to Edmonton or Calgary or even Vancouver to be with Billy and Nat, but now—now my future is uncertain.

"Not good enough! Again!" Coach Leblanc screams at us.

A collective groan erupts from my teammates, a few glares are shot in my direction. I don't blame them; my head hasn't been on the practice all morning. Instead, I've been thinking about Nella and Caterina, and how difficult it was to leave them last night after we tucked in Cat. My muscles ache and my body is coated in sweat by the time coach releases us for the day. Grayden and Chase flank my sides, both looking at me questioningly.

"Dude, what's going on with you lately?" Grayden asks.

"I don't know, man." I lie.

They let it pass, but I know I need to either get my head in the game or quit so my team can have a quarterback that doesn't have his head up his ass.

The atmosphere in the locker room is full of tension. My team knows I'm not giving them my all and they rightfully resent me for it. I'm shocked that no one has challenged me on it until now, I think it's because until summer training started, I have never let them down like this before. Their tolerance isn't going to last.

I pack my duffel bag and sling it over my shoulder, but before I can make my escape I hear my name.

"Jacobs, get your ass in here." Coach Leblanc's head disappears back into his office. Every one of my teammates watches me as I cross the room, step through the doorway, and shut the door behind me.

My ass hasn't even connected with the hard wood seat of the chair opposite him before he starts to scold me.

"When Sanderson told me about his team, I was expecting a competent quarterback. One whose love of the game was only outshone by his sense of teamwork and skill on the field. I have been waiting for that man to appear on the field for close to four months now."

I open my mouth to speak, but he holds his hand up silencing me. For the next forty-five minutes, he reprimands me for every single thing I've let my team down on. He actually has a list that he checks off as he goes.

"I'm suspending you for one week. When you return, you either need to shape up or you're done. It's unfair for the rest of your team to pick up your slack." He doesn't bother saying anything else as his cell rings and he answers it.

Grabbing my bag, I let myself out. The locker room is empty, which I'm grateful for; I don't want to deal with the knowing looks.

Everything is coming to a head and I have a lot of decisions to make. That can wait. Right now, I just want to get home, shower, and head over to Nella's.

CHAPTER 20

Nella

CARTER IS CRAWLING around on the ground chasing Cat. She's got that deep belly laugh going on. He's definitely a natural with her, his experience with his niece shining through as they play.

Since he walked in the door a few hours ago, he's done everything from helping prepare her snack, changing her diaper, and playing with her. The look on Cat's face when he walked in the door made my heart stutter before it took off at double its usual pace.

Cat comes running towards me, looking behind her as Carter chases her, and crashes to the ground. Her eyes widen as she takes a deep breath before exhaling a scream that could shatter a glass.

Carter is immediately at her side, his face white as he picks her up and cradles her to his chest. His eyes meet mine pleadingly when she continues to cry. "She must have really hurt herself! I can't believe I made her fall, we need to take her to a doctor."

Smiling at him, I hold out my arms for her. He hands her over and watches me set her on her feet. When her blue eyes look at me, the big crocodile tears tracking down her cheeks, I brush my thumb down her nose. "You're okay, baby girl. Where does it hurt? Here?" I lift her and kiss her belly. "Or here?" Setting her back down, I kiss her nose.

By the time I'm done, she's laughing again and running to her sandbox. Carter lifts me to my feet as we walk across the grass to sit on the wooden bench Ryan built for me.

"That was amazing! I can't believe I lost my head, I've seen Nat fall enough times to know kids can handle a lot." He drapes his arm over the back of the bench, pulling me into his side.

"It's easy to panic. Just because I'm calm on the outside, it doesn't mean the inside isn't freaking out."

"You're so incredible." Carter's lips brush against mine. If it wasn't for Caterina playing a few feet away, I would be crawling into his lap and finishing what we started yesterday.

By the time Caterina is down for the night and we're sitting on the couch watching a movie, I'm strung so tight Carter keeps glancing over at me in concern.

"You're really tense, are you okay?"

"Yeah—I was just thinking maybe you could spend the night . . . I know you have football in the morning, so I understand if you would rather sleep in your own bed instead of having to wake up at an ungodly hour to make it back to campus on time, it was just an idea."

He chuckles at my rambling. "I was hoping you would invite me to stay, I have a bag packed and waiting in my car. And as for football—Coach Leblanc hasn't been happy with my performance and suspended me for a week."

"Oh no. Carter, I'm so sorry."

"If I'm being honest with myself, I don't care. I haven't enjoyed playing since the end of the season; I think it's time to quit and let someone else take my place, someone who will give their all." His words and the look in his eyes are conflicting. It's obvious that while he may not be enjoying football anymore, it scares him to let such a huge part of his life go.

"Even so, it can't be an easy decision to make."

"It's easier now. I would rather have the time to spend with you and Caterina, especially since you may not be on campus, than play football for another year. I won't have time once I'm done with my Bachelors of Science."

"Have you started applying for practicum placements yet?" Leaning forward, I shut off the movie we're not even watching. "Isn't the deadline September fifth?"

He takes my hand and pulls me onto his lap. One of his hands rest on my hip, while the other plays around with my hair. "I like the dark, but I miss the auburn. The way the red would shine in the sun."

"You're avoiding the question."

"I haven't applied. If I don't get into Parkland's program, I will end up at a clinic in Edmonton or Calgary. My applications are ready to go, but I'm worried. I don't want to be that far away from you and Caterina." He smiles at me, but it doesn't meet his eyes.

"It's what you want to do and the experience will help you get into your Doctorate of Physical Therapy degree. Send in the applications." I shift my position on his lap so I'm straddling him.

His hands run up and down my arms, his eyes searching mine. "I just got you back in my life, and I'm just getting to know Cat. I don't want to give that up."

Shaking my head, I give him a soft smile. "Who knew you were such a softie? It's just for a summer and then you will be back here. Besides, I would be surprised if you didn't get accepted into Parkland's program."

He doesn't say anything, but I can see he's overthinking, dwelling on what could go wrong. What he doesn't realize is that I've already waited for two years and while a summer away from him would suck, I don't doubt that we can make it through.

His eyes lift to focus on mine when I slide my hips forward and lean down to kiss him. As I run my hands over his shoulders and into his hair, deepening the kiss for a brief moment, I feel a surge of confidence. Shifting back, I stand and hold my hand

out. He shoves up from the couch and links his fingers with mine, following me through the house as I lock up and shut off all the lights.

Instead of letting him dwell on his worries, something I know is not helpful, I lead him to my room and close the door behind us.

The moon is full and bright, its glow filling the room with a soft light. Turning, I step into his arms and wrap my arms around his neck. His eyes are dark as he leans down to meet my lips in a kiss so soft and sweet that it shoots straight to my heart. When his hands wrap into my hair, tilting my head back to deepen the kiss, my brain short circuits and I push him until his back hits the wall.

Stepping back, I lock eyes with him as I pull my shirt over my head. It briefly crosses my mind to cover the small silver stretch marks, but the thought is fleeting. I'm not ashamed of my body. Besides, I've been working out with Andie for almost a year, and now working here on the ranch, I'm in better physical shape than ever.

Carter watches with his hands pressed into the wall as I strip off the rest of my clothes, walk backwards to the bed and inch my way to the center of the mattress. Lifting one hand, I hook a finger at Carter, beckoning him to join me.

Little trails of heat follow the path of his eyes as he devours me. I can't even enjoy watching him strip down because I can't tear myself away from the desperate want in his eyes.

Want that is just for me. And it makes me feel so incredibly sexy that I find my hand traveling up my hip, over my stomach, to my peaked nipple and roll it between my thumb and forefinger.

Carter groans, his hands faltering at the waistline of his boxer briefs, his eyes locked on my fingers. Glancing down, I feel my pussy pulse with need when I see his erection straining against the material constraining it. Licking my lips, my hand moves down my body to between my legs where my body aches for him.

Every muscle feels tight, every nerve firing as my body craves him. Brushing my fingertips over my wetness, I circle my clit with one finger, little gasps escaping from my lips.

He finally drops his boxer briefs and stalks over to me, prowling up the bed until his body is hovering over mine. He braces himself on one elbow as he snakes his hand between us to rest on my hand which is frozen between my legs. He grasps it, brings it up our bodies, and sucks my fingers into his mouth.

"I never got to taste you the first time." His voice is rough as he pins my hand above my head, kissing me in a way that hints at what his tongue will be capable of. "It's time to change that."

Chewing on my lower lip as he kisses his way down my body, I tense a little when he kisses my lower stomach. Through the haze of arousal and sparks from the chaos of feelings, reality hits that he will have his face planted in my most intimate area. Since that night, I've explored my own body, I know what I like, but that's not something I've ever experienced.

Carter looks up at me, a lazy smile on his face. "Nella, trust me."

"I do." The words are hoarse, my head falling back as he moves between my legs and nips my inner thigh. He trails kisses all over, except where I need him most. I'm so wet, my body aching for the release I know is coming.

The moan that erupts from my throat the moment his tongue strokes over me before his lips wrap around my swollen clit is loud. So loud, I think I faintly hear Grace say, "Oh my."

"Nell, you're going to wake up the entire house." Carter's voice is thick, low, and pleased. He doesn't wait for me to respond before his tongue continues its assault.

And an assault it is. His arms wrap around my waist to hold me still, my body out of my control as it writhes with the pleasure coursing through me. Throwing my pillow over my face, I bite into the material as an orgasm rips its way through me.

I feel Carter kiss his way up my wrecked body, before the

pillow is tugged away from my face and tossed aside. I'm a quivering mess, my face flushing as he looks down at me. I blush even deeper when I see the way his lips glisten with *me*.

Before I can sort myself out, his lips are on my neck, his cock nestled between my legs. Wrapping my hands in his hair, I whimper with need as he slowly presses into me. Every inch is sweet torture. Through the ringing in my ears, I hear myself begging him. His name a whispered request for all of him. His body. His mind. *His heart.* I want it all. He's had all of me for so long, I want all of him in return.

Our lips meet in a slow, exploratory kiss as he starts to move. As we find our rhythm, I feel cherished by him. When our lips part, he looks down at me with a soft smile, a smile that makes my heart swell. His hips begin to move faster, bringing us closer to that edge, and I can't look away. I can't escape the depths of those blue eyes, those eyes that can't seem to look away from me either.

It's in those eyes that I see he's just as impacted by me as I am him, the look he's giving me is a look I can feel deep inside my soul and it's as calming as dipping my toes into a tranquil lake on a hot day.

When those delicious waves start running over me, I bury my face into Carter's shoulder to prevent myself from crying out. His release follows mine, the rumbling sounds coming from deep in his chest only make my orgasm so much better.

He gently pulls out of me, his gorgeous ass disappearing into my bathroom before he returns with a warm cloth for me. Instead of being embarrassed, the moment feels intimate and I beam at him as he settles in next to me, pulling me into his chest.

We don't speak, just enjoy the quiet moment. Everything perfect. We took care of the awkward conversation about protection and previous partners—for him—out of the way earlier today.

Chuckling quietly, I blush when Carter pulls away to smile at me. "What's so funny?"

"I was just thinking of our conversation earlier."

"You mean the conversation that made me feel like a man whore?"

"You're not. And no, I guess I was laughing at the fact I had the balls to bring it up."

He growls when I bite him on the shoulder, his lips capturing mine in a kiss that's the perfect combination of sweet and rough. "Thank you for not making me feel like shit about all of that."

Humming, I curl into him again, my eyes falling shut as exhaustion finally wins out. "It's always been you. The rest doesn't matter." The words are a whisper, I'm not even sure if he hears them, but it feels good to say them out loud.

As I drift off, I finally feel free of the anxiety I've clung to, the fear of being exposed, and hold fast to the courage and confidence that surges forward. I don't want to hide anymore. I don't want to hold back.

I want to live.

And love.

And be free of regrets.

I wake up to Carter talking. Keeping my eyes closed, I listen to his deep voice. When he falls silent, Caterina's few words mixed in with toddler speak fills the silence. With a smile, I open my eyes and sit up with my hand pressed to my chest to ensure the sheet keeps me covered.

"Good morning." Carter strides across the room, leans on the bed, and gives me the sweetest kiss.

"Good morning."

"I hope you don't mind, I woke up early and heard her stirring. I thought you might like the chance to sleep in, so I changed her and got her ready for the day." He looks a little nervous, like he's waiting for me to get upset at him behaving like a father.

Leaning into him, I press my lips to his. "Of course I don't mind."

The crown of Cat's head appears next to the bed, her arms lifting as she asks to be lifted up. The shift on Carter's face is immediate as he obligingly lifts her onto the bed so she can come and cuddle up against me.

I can't help the laugh that escapes when I see her hair. Carter attempted to put in a ponytail the way I had it yesterday, but it's crooked and looks adorable.

Cat hears me laugh and starts laughing too, causing Carter to join us despite the light blush on his cheeks.

He shrugs, ruffling my bed head as he sits next to me on the bed.

Caterina looks over at Carter as she starts to talk again, and watching him listen to her nonsensical story is the sexiest thing I've ever seen. He's paying attention, even though there is no way he can understand what she's telling him.

We sit in my room playing and talking, looking every bit like the family I've dreamed of since I found out I was pregnant. Every so often Carter smiles at me when Caterina does something funny, like when she was trying to stand on her head, and the look makes me feel like I've given him the best gift in the entire world.

My reminder beeps on my cell when it's time for me to get ready for work, so Carter takes Cat out to the kitchen to eat breakfast while I get ready for the day.

As I throw on a pair of jeans and a tank top, I wait for my anxiety to surface. The rush of worry that usually finds me when I'm going through my monotonous morning routine. When I feel nothing but some lingering aches from last night and an eagerness to start my day, I do a little wiggle and smile.

A smile that stays with me when I join my little family in the kitchen to inhale a quick breakfast. One that stays with me as I make the quick walk to work. And it grows even more when Lia gives me a knowing smirk and we dive right into our day.

CHAPTER 21

CARTER

CAT'S PLAY ROOM in the basement is a disaster. We've been downstairs for two hours playing, two hours since Nella walked out the door to go to work, and Caterina just went nuts. I haven't seen her this hyper, but she's all over the place and so is every single one of her toys.

Footsteps warn me that Grace is approaching, and I know by the grin on her face that I look as overwhelmed as I feel. I'm so out of my element. I don't know whether I should try to contain Cat's energy, or just let her continue her path of destruction.

Rather than giving me some insight, Grace's smile just widens. "I'm running to town. I let Nella know I won't be home tonight. She should be home around four."

With a "have fun" chuckled at me as she makes her way back upstairs, I glance at the time on my cell. It's not even eleven o'clock. I thought the amount of respect I have for Nella and Grace was already maxed out, but I was wrong.

With a hand through my hair, I sit next to Cat as she spreads her blocks around her and starts to build. Containing this seems like a battle I can't win, instead I decide to follow her lead and just enjoy my time with her.

We've moved onto playing some musical instrument when

my phone beeps at me. Sliding it out of my pocket, I grin when I see its Nella checking in on me.

Nella: How's it going?

Me: Good. She's playing with some piano type toy and getting mad at me any time I try and put her toys away.

Nella: Lol. Ah, it's one of those days.

She starts typing again, the little dots blinking at me. Glancing over to Cat when the music stops, I watch her crawl into her play house and sit on the mound of pillows. Her fist is in her mouth as she fiddles with a wall of gadgets that Ryan built for her. There are switches, buttons, levers, and a ton of other moveable gadgets screwed into the board.

Nella: Since Grace is gone tonight, I thought it might be a good night to invite everyone over, let them meet Cat . . . what do you think?

Me: I think everyone will be thrilled. What can I do?

I join Cat in her tent, pushing buttons and telling her what each thing is. I have no idea what I'm doing, but it seems like a good idea.

Nella texts me ten minutes later that everyone will be over around six, followed by a list of things she wants to get done before they come over. It's obvious that she's nervous, even though we both know that our friends will take all of this in stride.

Cat starts screaming, drawing my attention from my phone. Her hand is clutched to her chest, giant tears rolling down her cheeks, and it makes me feel like the shittiest dad. I shouldn't have been so focused on my phone, I should have been paying more attention to Cat.

Gathering her in my arms, my heart starts to pound when she won't let me look at her hands and her cries become even louder. I feel like I'm going to choke on the air I'm breathing as I try to remain calm.

What the fuck do I do?

Lifting Cat to her feet, I crouch down so I'm at eye level. "You're okay, Cat." The words come out in a stressed coo, her eyes lock on mine as she continues to cry.

Inhaling a deep breath, I try again with a more soothing tone. "Let me see your hand. May I kiss it better?"

I reach out, my fingertips wrapping gently around her closed fist. This time she lets me take it. I kiss her hand with big loud smacks until her tears stop. Picking her up, I remember Nella blowing a raspberry on her cheek to distract her from being upset, so I do the same and soon Cat is laughing.

Inspecting her hand, I breathe a sigh of relief when I see she's fine. Swinging her into the air, I make airplane noises as I carry her upstairs to feed her lunch.

By the time Nella walks in the door at ten after four, I'm positive I look like a mess, but when she sees me and Cat on the floor the smile that shines on me is one I would gladly be a mess every day just to see it again.

"How did it go today?" She drops down onto the floor next to us, grabbing Cat around the waist and scooping her into her arms. Cat giggles as Nella plants kisses all over her face.

"It was challenging and amazing and eye-opening and exhausting. I loved it." Despite the challenges of the day, the near panic attacks, I wouldn't change anything about it.

Her dark eyes are warm as she looks at me. "I'm so glad. Most days she's easy, but every now and again she has a busy day where all you can do is try and keep up."

"So it wasn't just for me?"

She chuckles and shakes her head. Caterina is playing happily by herself, finally calm after the day we had.

While Cat is playing, we get up to start tidying the house as Nella tells me about her day.

"Beau went home today. He was the sweetest boy and it was awesome to watch him get better. His owner was so happy with my work, she asked for me specifically to come out once a week to maintain his massage therapy."

I've never seen anyone talk about their work with as much passion and enjoyment as Nella. In high school, she always hid behind a smile, it makes me incredibly happy to see a genuine one on her face.

Tossing the dish towel onto the counter, I wrap my arm around her waist and pull her into me. Leaning down, I capture her lips with mine. Every thought I have when I kiss her, or touch her, or even just spend time with her, is terrifying in a way I crave.

I love being with her and knowing she could destroy my world but trusting that she won't. It's something I've never let myself experience before. I just can't tell her how much I care about her yet, I need to deal with my fuck face of a father first.

Nella's chest rises and falls quickly as she tried to catch her breath. Her arms wrap around me tightly, her cheek resting against my chest. Looking down at the crown of her head, I hold her close.

When the doorbell rings, Nella looks up at me, licking her lips. "Are you ready for this?"

"Don't be dramatic. It's just another evening with our friends."

She smacks me in the chest, laughing as she rushes to the door when the bell rings again. She opens the door and the entry way fills with voices and a flurry of activity as the girls come in first hugging Nella.

I hold Cat in my arms as we both watch the house fill up. Everyone is so distracted by catching up with Nella that they haven't noticed me and Cat.

Silence falls as Nella comes to stand next to us and seven sets of eyes follow her to me.

"Holy shit." Andie is the first to speak, and in true Andie fashion she doesn't filter. "Nella—Cat looks just like . . ."

"Carter," Lucas finishes.

Laughing, I put Cat in her high chair. "Nothing gets past you guys."

Nella elbows me before she sits on her seat next to Cat as I go into the kitchen to grab snacks while Nella fills in the holes of our story. Every single piece of it.

Everyone gapes at us as I load the table with food before taking my seat on Cat's other side and set her bowl down with snacks.

Andie finally breaks the silence as she stands up and holds her hands out. "That is so cool! It's like a modern fairy tale."

And just like that we start catching up on everything else.

After a couple of hours, I stand to tuck Cat in, leaning down to kiss Nella before lifting our daughter and carrying her from the room.

A collective "aww" follows me into Cat's room. Her eyes getting heavy as I change her and put on her pajamas.

Kissing her forehead, I lay her down just as Nella comes in to say goodnight.

"That was easier than I thought." Her words are soft as she links her fingers with mine. "I had it built up in my mind, how telling everyone was going to go. Even though our friends have always been incredibly supportive, the chance that we would be the ones to tip the scale worried me."

Lifting her hand to my lips, I kiss her knuckles. "I think they took it well because, despite everything, we haven't had any major blow-ups."

"Thankfully. I've had enough drama to last me a lifetime."

Tugging on her hand, we close Cat's door and head back to the kitchen where we rejoin our friends. The rest of the night passes quickly until we're standing on the front porch watching their taillights fade down the driveway.

"Spend the night?" Nella pulls me back into the house.

I kick it shut behind me, locking up. "Hell yeah."

Nella's hands press into my chest, her lower lip caught between her teeth as she lowers herself down onto my cock. She moves her body, riding me, and I can't take my eyes off her.

Her hair is messy in the sexiest way, tangled from her fingers gripping it while I went down on her. Her smooth, tan skin flushed with arousal. Her eyes are hooded as she watches me. Everything about her is sexy.

Throaty moans fill the room as she throws her head back, moving faster. Sliding my hand up her thigh, I circle her clit with my thumb as her pussy starts clenching around me.

"God, yes." Her words flip a switch in my brain, I grab her by the waist and flip her onto her back, slamming back into her.

I pin her hands above her head with one hand while bracing myself with the other. Nella starts mumbling nonsense, her head shaking back and forth, as I move. She cries out when her body tenses, her pussy clenching around my dick pushes me over the edge with her.

Sex with Nella is incredible. Now I understand why Lucas and Dax don't talk about their sex lives the way Dean and I do. I've never been with someone who meant more to me than getting off, well, except for the first time with Nella, and there is no comparison, there is no way in hell I would brag about Nella to my buddies.

Collapsing onto the bed next to Nella, I pull her into my arms.

"I love you, Carter." She plants a kiss on my chest, snuggling in close.

Every muscle in my body tenses. I'm crazy about her, in fact, I love her too. When I go to speak the words, they won't come out. I can't say them back until one last obstacle is out of the way. *My father.* I know Nella doesn't need that, but I do.

You're such an idiot. I'm so full of shit. Saying the words means I'm allowing her to have the last piece of me. I know myself well enough to realize that this is my attachment issues rearing their ugly heads, but no matter how hard I try to force the words out they won't come.

Nella stays put in my arms for a few more minutes, the silence in the room thick with my unsaid words, before she rolls out of bed with a sigh and a sad smile.

Her bathroom door closes and the shower turns on. I know I should follow her in there. I know I should join her in the shower, wrap my arms around her, and tell her I love her too, but like a coward I throw on my clothes and head out into the kitchen.

Grace grins at me from where she is feeding Caterina. "Good morning. Are you spending the day here again?"

"I need to talk to my football coach, my week to decide what I want is up, and then make a trip to see my jerk of a father." I sit next to Cat and make growly noises as I pretend to eat her hand. She laughs hysterically. "I can see why Nella had such a hard time, the idea of not seeing her for a couple days really sucks."

"It's definitely better now. This was the best thing she could have done for herself."

Before I can respond I hear Nella's bedroom door close. Turning my head, I watch as she comes into the kitchen. She smiles at the three of us sitting at the table before grabbing a bowl and pouring herself some cereal.

Grace stands, letting Nella take her usual spot next to Cat. She stares down at her bowl taking a couple of bites before she finally lifts her head and meets my eyes. The look in them nearly crushes me. It's like someone turned out the light.

Grace sits back down with a fresh cup of coffee.

I jump out of my seat and round the table. I can't just sit there and not do anything, but I know my actions won't make up for my silence. Wrapping my arms around Nella, I kiss her neck.

"I need to head out if I'm going to be on time for my meeting with Coach. I will call you later."

She tilts her head to kiss me. "Okay. Good luck." There is a

pause as I almost hear her swallow the words she spoke this morning.

With one last kiss, I tweak Cat on the nose, and then I'm out the door. I can't tear my eyes away from the closed door of the house as I turn my car around. The past week has been the best one of my entire life.

CHAPTER 22

Nella

"YOU'VE BEEN MOPEY all day. What's going on?" Lia releases the mare she's working on, slinging the halter over her arm, and walks over to me.

"I told Carter I love him this morning. He didn't say it back. I'm not surprised, but I guess I was hoping after the week we've had he might say it back." I give Orlando one last cookie and take his halter off.

"Ouch, but you know how some guys are. Look at Alex when he found out I was pregnant. It will all work out." Lia hooks her arm through mine as we head into the cool sanctuary of our office.

"I know. I'm just being a girl. I forget sometimes that while I was pining for him, he wasn't in the same place." Dropping into my chair, I shrug my shoulders and give her an unconvincing smile.

"Okay, I get it. I'm dropping the subject." Lia walks over to the giant calendar on the wall next to our desks. "Now, we have ten new horses coming over the next three days. Three of them are in rough shape, I want to tag team those so I can train you in first aid. You're going to take four and I will take three of the less severe cases."

I jot down notes as she describes what we're working with, creating new files as we go through each one. The morning passes in a blur, it always does. When I first chose to go to university, I didn't have anything that called to me. This calls to me. When I think of going back to school, I don't feel a sense of excitement, just dread at the idea of not being here. Dread at the thought of giving up something so incredible. Dread at the idea of a career I am not passionate about.

"Lia—I want to stay here. I want to come on full-time. If I take any courses, I want them to be specific to enhancing the clinic and the services you offer here at the ranch."

The squeal that Lia lets out is piercing.

The door bangs open, Ryan standing in the frame as he looks around the room with his eyes narrowed. His fierce scowl clears when he sees us alone in the room, Lia's hands pressed together as she grins.

"What is going on?"

"Nella has decided to stay here full time!" Lia does a little wiggle. "Oh crap, now I have to pee."

Ryan and I chuckle as she races into the other room, her body twisting in weird ways.

"That's fantastic news." Ryan comes over and wraps his arm around me, giving me a one-armed hug. "I noticed your boyfriend leaving this morning. I was beginning to think he moved in."

Snorting, I shake my head. "He's not ready for that."

Ryan doesn't say anything, just gives me a sympathetic smile. He knows he's not the best for giving advice about committing, the man has no interest in settling down.

Lia comes back in, glowing. "We're clearing our schedule for the rest of the day and going riding. I want to celebrate."

"Lia, you know Alex will want to go with you," Ryan warns with a grin.

She waves her hand dismissively, grabs my wrist, and we're

out the door.

The entire time we're saddling our horses, I'm barely holding it together. Lia is watching out for Alex like a hawk. By the time we swing up into our saddles, tears are running down my face from laughing so hard.

"Laugh all you want, but the second the man found out I was pregnant, he's become so overprotective it's insane. I love that he cares so much, but Ollie will never do anything to hurt me." She nudges Ollie into a trot, leading us down a trail I've never ridden.

Eore follows, his ears flicking between Lia and me as we chat.

"Oh shit! I totally forgot to tell you. Alex and I are heading to Mistik Ridge to check out and pick up a horse. Apparently, someone abandoned it at the inn and the owner, Natasha, contacted me after she found our ranch on Google." Lia turns in the saddle, Ollie continuing to walk along the trail. "We will only be gone for a few days, but I need you to take over responsibility of getting the horses their supplements and what not."

"Of course. You know I will do whatever I can to help out."

"You're the best. You feel okay to be on your own for a few days?"

"Yeah, I think so. I can always ask Ryan to hold a horse for me if I need help."

She nods, her expression serious as she outlines what needs to be done. Pride fills me when there is nothing she mentions that surprises me.

As we ride, I tell her about my desire to learn how to train horses and to one day have my own horse. One of the things I love about working for Lia is that she's eager to help me achieve my aspirations.

"I will talk with Dane about having you shadow him in training from start to finish. Although, training is something that is never complete. Even with Ollie, I have to work him every week to make sure he stays on top of his training."

As Lia leads us to a small creek that winds throughout the property we fall silent. We ride along the water, the sun shining on it makes it look like shimmering diamonds. The soft sound of water flowing is soothing, and my shoulders relax.

The soft thud of our horses' feet, the sound of the water, and the birds chirping is better than any form of meditation. My mind is calm as I reflect on the past two years and finally on what happened with Carter this morning.

"I think this morning was probably harder on Carter than it was on me." Breaking the silence, I flinch when Lia startles in the saddle. Alex would kill me if anything happens to her.

"Why do you say that?" We come to a fork in the trail and she nudges Ollie in the direction to head back to the clinic.

"He's dealt with a huge life change. A kid, a baby momma, learning his father kept all of this from him, and, to top it all off, he's managing all of this while fighting his attachment issues. I'm sure the fact that he hurt me by not saying 'I love you' back is haunting him. It takes him a long time to trust people, to open up to them, and I closed myself off." Sighing, I reach forward to run my fingers over the smooth hair of Eore's neck.

"Sometimes it's easy to forget the struggles of others. From what you've told me about Carter, he's either figured out how to cope with his attachment or he's low on the spectrum. He will come around. He just needs to figure it out in his own way and on his own time. Can you be patient? Can you continue to tell him you love him and be okay with not hearing it back? Because that's what he needs." Lia's voice is soft, but her words strike me straight in the heart.

"You're right. Where did you learn so much about attachment?"

Lia blushes as she shrugs her shoulders. "When I first met Alex, Emma mentioned that he had attachment issues. I couldn't get him out of my head, so I read a bunch of books written by experts in the field. Alex's issues were more from fear, his parents were pretty messed up, but I find the topic fascinating so I still read books on it. You can see some of the same behavior in horses, and I've actually developed some rehabilitation strategies based off psychological research."

I'm stunned as Lia continues to meander through the winding trails that weave throughout the entire property.

Lia has taught me so much about myself in the months I've been with her. I admire how she craves knowledge and takes what she learns to enhance her business. It's because of Lia that I get to see my daughter every day. It's because of her open heart that I am developing a career I love. It's because of her that I no longer look at my bank account with a sense of dread. It's because of her that I'm in this place I know I'm meant to be.

"I don't know how I will ever be able to repay you for everything you've done for me and my family." My voice is hoarse as I whisper the words.

Lia spins Ollie to face me. Her brow furrows when I lift my hand to brush it over my eyes. "Hey, what is this?"

Dropping my gaze, I braid Eore's mane with trembling fingers. "I just—there is really no way to express what being here means to me. You took me under your wing, gave me your friendship, hired me for a job I'm still learning, and offered me a salary I'm nowhere near qualified enough yet to expect."

She pushes Ollie forward until he's right next to me, before taking my hand. "Listen to me. Everything you have here, you've earned. Our ranch is successful because everyone who is here is dedicated to it. It didn't take me long to recognize your potential. Besides, with you working alongside me, I can more than double the number of horses I have here at one time. I know you feel like you need to prove yourself, but you don't. You're part of our family now, and we take care of our family."

By the time we've returned Eore and Ollie to their pasture, I'm smiling again. Today has been an overwhelming day of emotions. I think some of my own issues surfaced this morning. I accepted a long time ago that Mom and Dad didn't want a second child, but today when Carter didn't tell me he loved me

back it brought me back to the days when my parents would just dismiss me.

What began as a celebratory ride became the chance to get the clarity I need.

CHAPTER 23

CARTER

THE SOUND OF my knock on coach's office door echoes in the empty locker room. The sound rings hollow in my ears. I thought after fifteen years of playing football this moment would feel more—impactful.

Coach's stern face greets me when the door swings open. He doesn't say a word as he turns on his heel and walks back to his seat. Shutting the door behind me, I sit across from him and lean forward on my elbows.

"I'm done. I've thought about this a lot over the past week, but I think my mind has been made up for a long time. Football just isn't important to me anymore, not the way it used to be."

Coach looks taken aback by my bluntness, but there is no sense in dancing around reality. This is just step one.

"I have to admit when I told you to take the week, I didn't think you would come back and quit. I thought maybe you just needed a break." He leans back in his chair and crosses his arms. He seems disappointed in my decision.

"Coach, I love football, but I'm ready to focus on other things. Within the past couple of months, I've gone through some life changing events, including finding out I am a father. I need to prioritize. Coleson is a fantastic quarterback, I would

argue he's better than me because his heart is in the game."

"Okay." He stands, but then sits on the edge of his desk. "I think the team would like you to share the news."

Rising to my feet, I meet his gaze. "I appreciate that, but if I'm being honest, I think they already know. I don't want to make a huge deal out of it, just put Coleson in. The guys know how to reach me if they want."

Coach nods, his lips pursed in a thin line, but he doesn't say anything as he holds his hand out to shake mine.

I feel his eyes on me as I walk out the door and shut it behind me.

I don't look back as I leave this part of my life behind.

Nella: How did it go?

Me: Good. It's the right choice. I knew as soon as I walked into the locker room and didn't feel any sense of doubt. It's just not where I need to be anymore.

Nella: I'm glad.

Nella: Cat was asking for you when I got home.

Me: Really? That makes my day.

Nella: How long are you planning on staying in Edmonton?

Me: I guess it depends on how it goes tomorrow. I will let you know for sure as soon as I do.

Nella: Okay. Want to come straight here after? Or do you need to go home?

Me: I want to come see you and Cat. I want to spend as much time with you two before school starts.

Nella: I love you.

Opening the door to my father's office without bothering to knock, I can hardly contain my gag reflex when I see his receptionist practically sprawled across his desk. She doesn't appear to be more than a few years older than me, her top is unbuttoned to show off large tits, and by the way she pulls herself away from the desk, dragging bright pink nails down his arm, it's apparent they're fucking.

He's disgusting.

She shuts the door behind her as she exits the room, my father's eyes on her the entire way.

"She's basically useless, but that ass makes it worth it." He leans back in his chair, pressing the tips of his fingers together as his usual sneer appears. "What are you doing here?"

Instead of answering, I pull out the contract he made Nella sign, stalk over to his desk, and slam it onto the mahogany surface.

His glances down at it, his eyes narrowing as he looks back up at me. "I see that little bitch got her claws into you."

Slamming my palms onto his desk, I ignore the sting as I lean forward. "Shut your fucking mouth. You don't get to say one thing about Nella. Now listen here, we're going to revise this contract per these conditions,"—yanking an envelope out of my back pocket, I slide it forward—"or we're going to have a problem. I'm positive you don't want this going public, it may impact the deal you're working on with the city currently."

"Are you seriously blackmailing me?" He smirks, ignoring the paper in front of him. "I was trying to save you. Save you from falling into the same situation your brother's mother tried to land me in. That little twit meant nothing."

His words make my heart stop, but outwardly I'm calm. I know what he's trying to do, but I won't let him distract me.

"No, I'm simply giving you the option to avoid a very public trial, because I've spoken with a lawyer and I have the grounds to sue you, as does Nella, based on this contract and the information you've withheld." Backing away from the desk, I don't lose eye contact as I straighten my jacket. "You have until the end of the day to decide. Keep that copy of the contract, we have the original."

Without waiting for him to open his foul mouth, I leave his office without a backward glance. I don't know whether he will agree to my new terms, or if he will chance the bad press, but I'm ready to fight him on this. The man owns the largest development company in Alberta, his resources are vast, but I'm banking on his desire to keep his personal life out of sight from his investors.

Once I'm in my car, I open the last text from Nella. *I love you.* Those words and the way they make me feel, the way she makes me feel, still terrify me. But when I read them again, the feeling of wanting to run away, run away from the chance of being hurt, is gone. In fact, I want to leave this city and go home to her and Cat.

Ignoring that urge, I tap on my brother's phone number and call him.

"I thought you'd forgotten me." Billy's laughing voice grounds me for a moment and I smile.

"Never." Backing out of my parking stall, I merge into the onslaught on rush hour traffic. "I've just been—distracted."

"You sound weird, what's going on?"

With a deep breath, I say, "I have a daughter. Dad forced Nella to sign a contract stating she would never contact me about said daughter, but I found out. I quit football. I met Cat, she has my eyes. I just left dad's office and told him if he doesn't agree to the terms of a new contract I had drawn up, I will take him to court. Nella told me she loves me and I didn't say it back. For the first time, I want to commit because I love her too, even though it scares the shit out of me. How could you not tell me you have a different mother?"

The crackle of static is the only sound in my car as I navigate traffic to my hotel. Finally, I hear Billy say something to Natalie before a door shuts.

"That's a lot of information to process." He clears his throat, but doesn't say anything for a moment. "I'm sorry I never told you about my mother. When Dad wouldn't give her the money she wanted to look after me, she left me and Dad had no option but to take responsibility for me. He resented me for being born, he resented me because he was engaged to Lucia when Mom found out she was pregnant. It almost ruined their relationship. Lucia raised me as her own, but still told me about my mother when I was old enough to know. She told me that my mom loved me, but she was scared to raise me as a single mother. I know now that it was a lie, but she just wanted me to feel loved."

I don't reply as I shoulder check and switch lanes to merge into the parking lot of my hotel. It's sad that his mom didn't want him, but selfishly I'm glad because it led to our close relationship, but . . ."That still doesn't explain why you didn't tell me. Especially in the past couple of years."

"I guess the only reason I have is because I was worried it would change our relationship."

"You're my brother, having different mothers doesn't change that." I park in my assigned spot, shutting my car off before I pick my phone up and hold it to my ear. The parking garage echoes with my footsteps as I hike to the elevator and punch the button to my floor.

There is a pause on his end, but I hear the sigh of relief. "Now—want to explain to me the rest of what you were saying? You have a kid? I have a niece? I need more information."

The elevator dings as the doors slide open. Crossing the hall, I cradle the phone against my shoulder as I slide the key-card in the door. "Do you remember Breanne, that quiet girl from high school I would walk home every once in a while?"

"Yeah. You had a one-night stand with her and then never saw her again until you realized the girl you can't get out of your head is her. I know all that."

"Well, she got pregnant that night. I guess she went to the house to tell me and Dad told her I wanted nothing to do with

her or the baby." I switch my phone to speaker as I toss my jacket onto the chair. I fill him in on the rest of the story as I strip down and change into sweats.

"Holy shit." Billy mumbles something unflattering about our father. "I don't even want to give that man any head space. I can't believe you have a kid! It sucks that I won't be able to meet her until Christmas."

"I have to admit I never thought this would be my life, but I actually love it. As scary as it is, I try to picture how I thought my summer would go and I just can't imagine it any other way."

A muffled crash sound through the phone. "Crap. I need to go. Keep me posted."

With a click Billy is gone. It's a relief to have talked things out with my brother a bit. Our friends are awesome, but with Nella being off campus now they're a little out of the loop. Besides, talking things out with Billy has always made things better.

Glancing at the time, I settle in for a long wait until I hear whether my father will agree to the new terms or force my hand.

> **Me:** I don't think I will make it out tonight. I have a feeling he's going to wait until the last possible moment to tell me whether or not he's agreeing to my new terms. Which means if I need my lawyer I won't be able to meet with him until tomorrow.
>
> **Nella:** New terms?
>
> **Me:** I didn't say anything, but I'm asking him to pay out the rest of the contract, plus an extra 80k to Grace. You both barely had enough to survive and it's the least I can do to make up for his deceit. Don't be mad, but I overheard you two talking about your debt and this would enable you to pay it off.
>
> **Nella:** I'm not mad—embarrassed, but not mad. My scholarships were enough for my tuition, dorm, and books. It wasn't enough for anything else that came up.

Me: I will take that burden away from you.

Nella: You know I don't expect that, but thank you.

Me: I will let you know what happens. I miss you and Cat.

Nella: We miss you too. I have a surprise for you when you get home. I love you.

It is one minute before the deadline I gave my father when my phone notifies me of an email. It's from his assistant. Opening the PDF she sent me, it's the newly drafted contract with the new terms—signed. Also attached is a confirmation of the deposit made to Nella's account and the information of where to pick the certified check up from for Grace.

Of course the bank is closed, forcing me to stay the night. He's so manipulative. But at least I can now be done with him. What I didn't tell Nella was that by signing he agrees to never contact her, myself, or anyone else in our family ever again.

I don't know why I allowed him so much power in my life until this point, but I'm done.

CHAPTER 24

Nella

"GRACE!" I SCREAM, my phone trembling in my hand. "Grace!"

My bedroom door slams open as I race out of my bathroom. "What's happening?"

Collapsing onto the floor, I clutch my phone to my chest and start to cry. My sister drops to the ground next to me and I try and speak through my sobs.

"He—he—signed."

Handing her my phone, I drop my face into my hands. Every part of me in trembling as the realization sinks in—all my debts will be paid. I won't have this burden hovering over me anymore.

Grace sputters as she sees the amount of money that was transferred to me this morning. Her lips move as she calculates the amount of child support I would have received by the time Cat is eighteen if nothing had changed. "I thought he was paying out the remainder of the child support balance—this is enough for that and to pay off our debts, with a ton left over. Did you know Carter was stipulating that?"

Shaking my head, I rub the palms of my hands over my eyes as I finally stop hyperventilating. "No, he wouldn't show me the

revised contract, he asked me to trust him and realistically I knew it couldn't get any worse."

She hands me back the phone, the balance in large black letters a beacon of hope.

Four hundred thirty-two thousand dollars.

Opening my text messages, I quickly type out a message and press send with trembling fingers.

> **Me:** It's too much. I don't even know what to do with that much money.

Grace pulls me to my feet when the sound of Cat's voice comes through the baby monitor. I tie my hair into a messy bun, tuck my phone in my pocket, and go about my morning routine as though my entire life has not just changed.

I'm exhausted by the time I kick my boots off at the end of the day. The rest of our intakes arrived today. Between the two of us, it took all morning to get them settled, and all afternoon to outline their treatment programs.

Carter still hasn't responded to my text, which worries me. My experience with Marshall is that he doesn't give without taking something in return.

He gave me child support, but took away my ability to reach out to Carter.

What did Carter have to give in order for him to sign a new contract? What did he have to sacrifice?

Caterina is looking out the living room window, her small hands gripping the window sill, when I come back from changing. "We Dada? We Dada?"

Her eyes are wide as she looks at me and points. She's been doing this since Carter left yesterday morning. She would look out and point asking over and over. Last night I taught her that Carter is "Dada" to surprise him when he comes back.

"Cat, what's this?" I hold up her stuffed monkey.

Distracted, she walks towards me holding her hand and tries to say monkey. It sounds more like she's saying "key," but she recognizes the word when I say it. She takes the toy and walks away with it, talking up a storm.

Sighing, I pull the curtain back and glance down the driveway before checking my phone again. The curtain falls back in place as I back away from the window and make my way to the kitchen to start cooking dinner.

Opening the fridge, I grab a head of lettuce and container of cut up veggies. When my phone beeps, I lunge for it, dropping the lettuce to the floor.

Disappointment fills me when it's Andie.

Andie: You being so far away sucks. We all miss you and it's been a tough adjustment not talking to you as often, so here's the deal. You're going to pick a night to come over for a girls' night. We're going to veg out, play games, gossip, and drink. You're going to spend the night. I swear, I will kidnap your sexy ass if you refuse.

Her text makes me laugh. Andie has softened in the last year since she and Lucas started dating, but she's still the hilarious woman I befriended almost a year ago.

Me: Okay. Can I let you know tomorrow?

Andie: I'm not happy that I need to wait, but fine.

We chat back and forth as I prepare dinner, distracting me from my worry. A girls' night sounds like just what I need. We used to get together every week, but I haven't spent any time with alone with my friends in a couple months.

An hour later I'm setting everything on the table when the sounds of tires on the gravel driveway sound through the open window. Grace takes the salad bowl from my hands so I can open the door.

Carter parks his car, grabs his bag from the back seat, and takes the steps two at a time before wrapping his arms around me.

I inhale the soft scent of his cologne, sinking into his embrace. "I was worried about you." The words are whispered. I don't want to ruin the moment, but I'm not okay with him leaving me hanging all day.

"I'm sorry. I was running around when your text came in and by the time I was done getting everything sorted out, all I could think about was getting on the road to see you." He leans back, cupping my cheek and tilting my head back so his lips can capture mine.

Every time we kiss is better than the last. I can feel his relief that his father has been dealt with. His relief to be back home. But what stands out even more is that there is a lack of restraint to this kiss that I now realize was missing before. Almost as though he is ready to admit what's growing between us, ready to admit that he loves me too.

"Dada!"

Carter freezes, and a slow smile spreads across my lips. I feel Cat's arms wrap around his legs. We part and both look down at her. Her blue eyes are glowing as she lifts her arms.

"Dada!"

Carter lifts Cat into his arms, his blue eyes glassy as she cups his cheeks. He looks over at me as we enter the house, his expression unreadable. "You taught her that?"

Flushing with happiness, I nod. "I wanted to surprise you."

He blinks a few times until the sheen disappears from his eyes. Once Cat is buckled into her highchair, he wraps me in his arms again, whispering into my hair how much that means to him.

Once we're seated at the table, Carter stops Grace from lifting the lids off the dishes.

"Before we eat, I have something for you."

Grace looks over at me, but I shake my head. I have no idea what he's up to. When he slides an envelope across the table, she stares at it for a moment before picking it up and sliding her finger under the seal.

Grace's eyes widen when she sees what's inside. "No. No, no, no."

She presses the seal closed and practically throws it across the table.

Carter pushes his seat back, grabs the envelope and moves to crouch down next to her. I cut up some food for Cat as I watch in confusion while he talks to her. Their conversation is hushed, but I can tell from Carter's tone that he won't accept "no" for an answer.

After several minutes of quiet arguing, I finally see Grace nod in agreement.

Before I can ask, she looks at me. "It's a certified check for eighty thousand dollars. To make up for the salary I couldn't earn over the past couple of years."

Carter meets my gaze with a soft look. "It's the least I can do after everything you have gone through. I don't ever want you to feel trapped again."

Dinner is a quiet affair. Grace appears on the verge of tears, and she rushes off to her room once she's done eating. Carter looks worried, but I reach across the table to squeeze his hand. "She's not used to having anyone really consider her. We've basically looked after each other for our entire lives. She's just overwhelmed."

As we clean up the kitchen, he fills me in on what happened with his father and everything he found out. Cat follows him around talking his ear off as toys build up in the middle of the floor.

By the time we shut the door to my bedroom, my previous exhaustion is gone. Carter lets out a tortured sound as I strip off my shirt, his lips crashing into mine as he lifts me and presses me into my closed bathroom door.

His tongue strokes mine as he deepens the kiss, an assault on the senses. My fingers work the buttons on his shirt until it's hanging open. I grind into him, my pussy aching for him.

When he sets me on the ground, I shove his shirt the rest of the way off until it falls to the floor. Before I can move to the button on his jeans, he has my hands pinned behind my back.

"Not yet." He kneels on the floor, his knuckles dragging across my skin as he pulls my jeans and panties to the floor. "Step out."

Licking my lips, I do as he says.

I gasp in a breath as his fingers start trailing soft paths over my sensitive flesh, teasing me as he presses fleeting kisses up my stomach, over my collarbone, and back to my lips. He leans down to press his forehead to mine.

"I love you, Nella."

The air rushes out of my lungs, but before I can reply, his lips are on mine again as he pushes me back until I'm falling on the bed. His jeans join the rest of the clothes on the floor, his weight pressing into the mattress as he kisses his way up my body.

Whispered words of love fill the room between each kiss and by the time he slowly pushes into me. He kisses me slowly and thoroughly, cherishing me as we move.

The only sound in the room is the sound of our breathing as we make slow love. We climax together, a quiet expression of a life changing moment.

Andie settles on the couch next to me, remote in hand as she hits play on the game of Mario Kart that we're playing.

I've played this game with her enough that I'm not half bad, but that doesn't mean I ever win. Grinning as she lets out a string of curses when her character spins out on the banana I threw down, I twist my hands as I get into the race.

"I am still having a tough time picturing Carter as a dad. I mean, I saw it with my own two eyes, that little girl already has him wrapped around her finger, but it's even more bizarre than my brother being a step-dad." Andie passes me, one hand reaching for a chip as the other drives her character.

She crosses the finish line and leans back with a smirk.

"Ugh." I follow behind, Ava and Peyton bringing in the third and fourth spots. Kensi tosses her controller to the couch, grumbling.

"I'm not surprised." Ava crosses her legs, setting a bowl of popcorn on her lap.

Scrolling to my most recent text from Carter, I show them the photo he sent me of him and Caterina. "He's with her right now. He took her swimming and now he's building her a blanket fort. He bought his own car seat and installed it himself."

"Let's face it, all our guys are amazing. We should fix Jaden up, get him out of his shell. He's so shy." Kensi plops down next to me, topping up all our margaritas before leaning back and wrapping her arm around me.

"Kensi, do you really think you should be setting anyone up when your love life is—to use your words—'a freaking disaster'?" Andie laughs as she sips her drink.

"Maybe playing matchmaker isn't a good idea—I don't want to be added to that list." Peyton chuckles, creating an X with her arms.

"We got distracted from the topic at hand." Andie looks over at me and winks. "Who else agrees that Carter is a sexy as fuck dad?"

A chorus of "hell yeah" makes me smile. My phone buzzes with another text, I open it to another photo and my smile widens.

It's from Grace. It's a photo of Carter and Cat asleep next to each other in the blanket fort. "You need to see this."

They lean in to look, cooing over how cute they look.

I smile as Andie loads another game, looking at the photo again before setting my cell aside. Life is so good. I will never need to speak to Marshall again. I paid off all my debts today and put the rest of the money the trust fund I was trying to put

money into for Cat. Carter loves me and is an incredible father.

An elbow jabs my side, interrupting my thoughts, a controller thrust into my hand. "Okay, focus. Enough boy talk, let's play video games like the awesome chicks we are."

CARTER
September

THE CROWD SCREAMS as the band finishes their set, but I am too busy sending Dax another text checking on Cat. Nella's hand finds mine, her fingers intertwine with mine, the tips barely reaching the phone.

"She's fine. This is the first real date we've had, just the two of us in weeks. Let's hit the food trucks and then make our way to the main stage. The Weeknd is up next."

Tucking my phone in my back pocket, I resist the urge to check Dax's response when I feel it vibrate. "You're right, I'm sorry."

I follow her as she weaves through the crowd, her eyes happy as she takes in the crowd. The sun shines on the gorgeous auburn, creating a halo at the crown of her head. I'm so happy she grew out the black hair dye. She's beautiful no matter what, but I love her natural color.

Once we're in the line for churros, I swing her around and kiss her. Stepping forward whenever someone clears their throat to inform us the line is moving.

Nella's chest heaves, her skin flushed, as she turns to order once we're at the front of the line. Wrapping my arms around her, we walk to the pick-up window to collect our treat.

"It's hard to believe that less than five months have passed since I found the tickets for this festival and we were excited to have a definitive date for our first meeting. So much has changed."

Smiling when I see she has some sugar on her upper lip, I lean down and kiss it away. "Things have changed, but I've never been happier."

"Especially since Parkland accepted you into their program. Have you told Jaden that you're moving out to the ranch yet?"

I can feel my face fall. Jaden and I have hardly spent any time together lately, and I know he's retreated even more into himself because of it. "No—I'm not second-guessing, I swear, I'm just worried about him."

"You're already not living there except for two nights a week, I think he knows what's coming," Nella says softly.

I nod, taking her garbage from her so I can throw it away. We join hands again, maneuvering through the crowd to make it to the main stage.

The noise is deafening, but she is relaxed as I wrap my arms around her and pull her into my chest. The days of anxiety attacks and hiding in the background are gone, the woman I love is a strong, confidant woman and I'm so proud of everything she has been accomplishing.

Leaning down to kiss her neck, my cock twitches when she tilts her head and moans. "I love you so damn much."

"I love you too."

The crowd cheers as The Weeknd appears on stage. I'm not paying attention as I nuzzle into Nella's neck. I could care less about the band; all I care about is this woman and our future together.

A future I never knew I wanted until her.

A future I want to last forever and a day.

ACKNOWLEDGEMENTS

Thank you so much to everyone who supported me through this book. Nella and Carter's story has evolved significantly since I first outlined their story. I felt there was more than what I had planned, and that's why it took so much longer than I intended.

Thank you to all the readers who have picked up this book. I appreciate you taking a chance on these two.

Thank you to my author friends, my editing team, my cover designer, and my formatter for your rock-solid support. I love you all.

Thank you, Christopher John, and Brendon Charles for the gorgeous cover photo.

A huge thank you to the bloggers who helped spread the word about The No Jock Rule. You are appreciated and valued.

Lastly, but definitely not least, thank you to my family for their support. It means the world to me.

ABOUT Ashley Erin

Ashley Erin lives in Alberta, Canada where winter and summer compete to take over. She wears flip flops as soon as it's above freezing, because her hatred of socks outweighs her dislike of snow. Her boyfriend stays with her despite a penchant for adopting rescued cats and dogs without permission. Their two dogs and four cats are spoiled rotten. When Ashley isn't writing, she is reading or working with horses.

Ashley is a self-published author of contemporary and new adult romance. Follow her on Facebook to keep up with her current and upcoming releases.